Agatha Raisin
and the
Potted Gardener

Agatha Raisin and the Potted Gardener

M. C. Beaton

ROBINSON
London

Constable & Robinson Ltd
3 The Lanchesters
162 Fulham Palace Road
London W6 9ER
www.constablerobinson.com

First published in the US 1994 by
St Martin's Press
175 Fifth Avenue, New York, NY 10010

First published in the UK by Constable,
an imprint of Constable & Robinson Ltd 2003

This paperback edition published by Robinson,
an imprint of Constable & Robinson Ltd 2005

A copy of the British Library Cataloguing in
Publication data is available from the British Library

ISBN 1-84529-136-0 (pbk)
ISBN 1-84119-775-0 (hbk)

Printed and bound in the EU

3 5 7 9 10 8 6 4

To Jane, with love

The author wishes to thank Nic Dicker of Batsford Garden Centre for his help in choosing plants for Agatha's 'instant garden'.

Chapter One

A mild, damp winter was edging towards spring when Agatha Raisin motored slowly homeward to the village of Carsely after a long holiday. She persuaded herself that she had had a wonderful time far away from this grave of a village. She had gone to New York, then to Bermuda, then to Montreal, and then straight to Paris, and so on to Italy, Greece and Turkey. Although she was a wealthy woman, she was not used to spending all that amount of money on herself and felt obscurely guilty. Before, she had nearly always gone on the more expensive arranged package holidays where she was with a group. This time she had been on her own. Carsely had given her the confidence, or so she had thought, to make friends, but she seemed to have spent a blur of weeks either in hotel rooms or in dogged solitary forays around the tourist sights.

But she would not admit she had had a lonely time any more than she would admit her prolonged absence had anything to do with her neighbour, James Lacey.

At the end of what she fondly thought of as 'my last case', she had drunk too much in the local pub with one of the women from the village and on returning home had made a rude gesture to James, who had been standing outside his cottage.

Sober and remorseful the next day, she had humbly apologized to this attractive bachelor neighbour and the apology had been quietly accepted. But the friendship had sunk to a tepid acquaintanceship. He talked to her briefly if he met her in the pub or in the village shop, but he no longer came round for coffee, and if he was working in his front garden and saw her coming along the lane, he dived indoors. So Agatha had taken her sore heart abroad. Somehow, away from the gentle influence of Carsely, her old character had reasserted itself, that is, prickly, aggressive and judgemental. Her cats were in a basket on the back seat. She had stopped at the cattery to pick them up on the road home. Despite the fact that she was still married, although she had not seen her husband for years, did not want to, and had practically forgotten his existence, she felt exactly like the spinster of the village, cats and all.

The village of Carsely lay quietly in the watery sunlight. Smoke rose from chimneys. She turned the car along the straggling main street, which was practically all there was of Carsely, except for a few lanes winding off it and a council estate on the outskirts, and turned sharply into Lilac Lane, where her thatched cottage stood. James Lacey lived next door. Smoke was rising from his chimney. Her heart lifted. How she longed to stop the car at his door and cry out, 'I'm home,' but she knew he would come out on the step and survey her gravely and say something polite like 'Good to have you back,' and then he would retreat indoors.

Carrying her cats, Boswell and Hodge, in their basket, she let herself into her cottage. It smelt strongly of cleaning fluid and disinfectant, her dedicated cleaning woman, Doris Simpson, having had free run of the place while Agatha had been away. She fed the cats and let them out, carried her suitcases out of the car and put her clothes in the laundry basket, and then took out a series of small parcels, presents for the ladies of Carsely.

She had bought the vicar's wife, Mrs Bloxby, a very pretty silk scarf from Istanbul. Longing for some human company, Agatha decided to walk along to the vicarage and give it to her.

The sun had gone down and the vicarage looked dark and quiet. Agatha suddenly felt a pang of apprehension. Despite her hard thoughts about Carsely, she could not imagine the village without the gentle vicar's wife. What if the vicar had been transferred to another parish while she, Agatha, had been away?

Agatha was a stocky middle-aged woman with a round, rather pugnacious face, and small, bearlike eyes. Her hair, brown and healthy, was cut in a short square style, established in the heyday of Mary Quant and not much changed since. Her legs were good and her clothes expensive, and no one, seeing her standing hopefully on the vicarage doorstep, could realize the timid longing for a friendly face that lay underneath the laminated layers of protection from the world which Agatha had built up over the years.

She knocked at the door and with a glad feeling heard the sound of approaching footsteps from within. The door opened and Mrs Bloxby stood smiling at Agatha. The vicar's wife was a gentle-faced woman. Her brown hair, worn in an old-fashioned knot at the nape of her neck, was streaked with grey.

'Come in, Mrs Raisin,' she said with that special smile of hers that illumined her whole face. 'I was just about to have tea.'

Having temporarily forgotten what it was to be liked, Agatha thrust the wrapped parcel at her and said gruffly, 'This is for you.'

'Why, how kind! But come in.' The vicar's wife led the way into the sitting-room and switched on a couple of lamps. With a feeling of coming home, Agatha sank down in the feather cushions of the sofa while Mrs Bloxby threw a log on the smouldering fire and stirred it into a blaze with the poker.

Mrs Bloxby unwrapped the parcel and exclaimed in delight at the silk scarf, shimmering with gold and red and blue. 'How exotic! I shall wear it at church on Sunday and be the envy of the parish. Tea and scones, I think.' She went out. Agatha could hear her voice calling to the vicar, 'Darling, Mrs Raisin's back.' Agatha heard a mumbled reply.

After about ten minutes, Mrs Bloxby returned with a tray of tea and scones. 'Alf can't join us. He's working on a sermon.'

Agatha reflected sourly that the vicar always managed to be busy on something when she called.

'So,' said Mrs Bloxby, 'tell me about your travels.'

Agatha bragged about the places she had been, conjuring up, she hoped, the picture of a sophisticated world traveller. And then, waving a buttered scone, she said grandly, 'I don't suppose much has been going on here.'

'Oh, we have our little excitements,' said the vicar's wife. 'We have a newcomer, a real asset to the village, Mrs Mary Fortune. She bought poor

Mrs Josephs's house and has made vast improvements to it. She is a great gardener.'

'Mrs Josephs didn't have much of a garden,' said Agatha.

'There's quite a bit of space at the front, and Mrs Fortune has already landscaped it and she has had a conservatory built at the back of the house on to the kitchen. She grows tropical plants there. She is also a superb baker. I fear her scones put mine to shame.'

'And what does Mr Fortune do?'

'There isn't a Mr Fortune. She is divorced.'

'How old?'

'It is hard to say. She is a remarkably good-looking lady and a great help at our horticultural society meetings. She and Mr Lacey are both such keen gardeners.'

Agatha's heart sank. She had nursed a hope that James might have missed her. But now it seemed he was being well entertained by some attractive divorcée with a passion for gardening.

Mrs Bloxby's gentle voice went on with other news of the parish, but Agatha's mind was too busy now to take in much of what she was saying. Agatha's interest in James Lacey was as much competitive as it was romantic. Since she had a great deal of common sense, she might even have accepted the fact that James Lacey was not interested in her at all, but the very mention

14

of this newcomer roused all her battling instincts.

The vicar's voice sounded from the back of the house. 'Are we going to get any dinner tonight?'

'Soon,' shouted Mrs Bloxby. 'Would you care to join us, Mrs Raisin?'

'I didn't realize it was so late.' Agatha got to her feet. 'No, but thank you all the same.'

Agatha walked back to her cottage and let the cats in from the back garden. She could not see much of the garden because night had fallen. She had put in a few bushes and flowers last year, Agatha being an 'instant' gardener – that is, someone who buys plants ready grown from the nursery. In order to get in on the act, she would need to become a real gardener. Real gardeners had greenhouses and grew their plants from seed. Also, she had better join this horticultural society.

With a view to finding out about the opposition, Agatha drove down to Moreton-in-Marsh the following day and bought a cake at the bakery and then drove back to Carsely and made her way to the newcomer's home, which was in an undistinguished terrace of Victorian cottages at the top of the village. As she opened the garden gate, she remembered with a pang of unease the last time she had pushed open this gate and had

15

entered the house to find that Mrs Josephs, the librarian, had been murdered. An extension had been built to the front of the house, a sort of porch made mostly of glass and filled with plants and flowers and wicker furniture.

Holding the cake, Agatha rang the bell. The woman who answered the door made Agatha's heart sink. She was undoubtedly attractive, with a smooth, unlined face and blonde hair and bright blue eyes.

'I am Agatha Raisin. I live in Lilac Lane, next to Mr Lacey. I have just returned from holiday and learned of your arrival in the village, and so I brought you this cake.'

'How very nice of you,' beamed Mary Fortune. 'Come in. Of course I have heard of you. You are our Miss Marple.' There was something in the way she said it and the appraising look she gave that made Agatha think she was being compared to the famous fictional character not because of that character's detective abilities but more because of her age.

Mary led the way into a charming sitting-room. Bookshelves lined the walls. Pot plants glowed green with health and a brisk log fire was burning. There was a homely smell of baking. Agatha could almost imagine James relaxing here, his long legs stretched out in front of him. 'I'll just take a note of your phone number,' said Agatha, opening her capacious handbag and taking out a notebook, pen and her glasses. She was not interested in getting Mary's phone number, only an excuse to put on her glasses and see if the newcomer's face was as unwrinkled as it appeared to be.

Mary gave her number and Agatha looked up and peered at her through her glasses. Well, well, well, thought Agatha. Thunderbirds, go! That was a face-lift if ever there was one. There was something in the plastic stretchiness of the skin. The hair was dyed, but by the hand of an expert, so that it was streaked blonde rather than being a uniform bleach job.

'I have heard you are a member of the horticultural society,' said Agatha, taking off her glasses and tucking them away in their case.

'Yes, and I pride myself on doing my bit for the village. Mr Lacey is a great help. You know Mr Lacey, of course. He's your neighbour.'

'Oh, we're *great* friends,' said Agatha.

'Really? But we must sample some of the cake you brought.' Mary stood up. She was wearing a green sweater and green slacks and her figure was perfect.

The doorbell rang. 'Talking of James, that'll be him now,' said Mary. 'He often calls round.'

Agatha smoothed her skirt. She realized she had not bothered to put on any make-up. Agatha knew there were lucky women who did not need to wear any make-up and that she was not one of that happy breed.

James Lacey came in and for a second a little flash of disappointment showed in his eyes when he saw Agatha. James Lacey was a very tall man in his mid-fifties. His thick black hair showed only a trace of grey. His eyes, like Mary's, were bright blue. He kissed Mary on the cheek, smiled at Agatha and said, 'Welcome back. Did you have a good holiday?'

'Mrs Raisin has brought a cake,' interrupted Mary. 'I'll make some tea while you two chat.'

James smiled at Mary without quite looking at her, as if he longed to look at her, but was as shy as a schoolboy. He's in love, thought Agatha, and wanted to get up and walk away.

She forced herself to talk brightly about her holidays, wishing she had some amusing stories to tell, but she had hardly talked to anyone and hardly anyone had talked to her.

Mary came back in bearing a tray. 'Chocolate cake,' she announced. 'Now we shall all get fat.'

'Not you,' said James flirtatiously. 'You don't have to worry.'

Mary smiled at him and James sent her back a shy little smile and bent his head over a slice of chocolate cake.

'I was thinking of joining the horticultural society,' said Agatha. 'When do they meet?'

'James and I are going to a meeting tonight, if you would like to come along,' said Mary. 'It's at seven thirty in the school hall.'

'I didn't know you were interested in gardening, Mrs Raisin,' commented James.

'Why so formal?' Agatha's bearlike eyes surveyed James. 'You always call me Agatha.'

'Well, Agatha, you've always just bought fully grown stuff from the nurseries before.'

'I've got time on my hands,' said Agatha. 'Going to do it properly.'

'We'll help you,' said Mary with an easy friendliness. 'Won't we, James?'

'Oh, absolutely.'

'Why did you decide to settle in Carsely, Mary?' Agatha felt the waistband of her skirt constricting her and put down her plate of half-eaten chocolate cake and shoved it away.

'I was motoring about the Cotswolds and took a liking to this village,' said Mary. 'So peaceful, so quiet. Such darling people.'

'Do you know someone was murdered in this house?' asked Agatha, determined to bring the conversation around to the murder case she had solved.

But Mary said quickly and dismissively, 'I heard all about that. It doesn't matter. These old houses must have seen a lot of deaths.' She turned to James and started talking about gardening. 'I've been pricking out my seedlings,' she said.

'What you do in the privacy of your home is your own affair,' said Agatha and gave a coarse laugh.

There was a frosty little silence and then Mary and James went on talking, the Latin names of plants Agatha had never heard of flying between them.

Agatha felt diminished and excluded. One part of her longed to get away and the other part was determined to hang on until James left.

At last, almost as if he knew Agatha would not budge until he left, James rose to his feet. 'I'll see you this evening, Mary.'

Mary and Agatha rose as well. 'I'll walk home with you, James,' said Agatha. 'See you this evening, Mary.'

Agatha and James went outside. When they had reached the garden gate, James suddenly turned and went back to where Mary was standing on the step. He bent his handsome head and whispered something to her. Mary gave a little laugh and whispered something back. James turned and came back to where Agatha was standing. They walked off together.

'Mary's an interesting woman,' said James. 'She is very well travelled. As a matter of fact, before coming here, she spent some time in California.'

'That would be where she got her face-lift,' said Agatha.

He glanced down at her and then said abruptly; 'I've just remembered, I must get something in for supper. Don't try to keep up with me. Must hurry.' And like a car suddenly accelerating, he sped off, leaving Agatha looking bleakly after him.

As she walked back home, Agatha was half inclined to forget about the whole thing. Let Mary have James. If that was the sort of woman who sparked him, then he wasn't for such as Agatha Raisin.

But competitiveness dies hard, and somehow she found that by the late afternoon she had ordered a small greenhouse complete with heating system and had agreed to pay through the nose to have the whole thing done the following week. She also bought a pile of books on gardening.

Before going to the horticultural society meeting, Agatha went along to the pub, the Red Lion. She wanted to come across just one person who did not like Mary Fortune. John Fletcher, the landlord, gave her a warm welcome and handed her a gin and tonic. 'On the house,' he said. 'Nice to have you back.'

Agatha fought down tears that threatened to well up in her eyes. It had been hell travelling alone. Single women did not get respect or attention. The little bit of kindness from the landlord took her aback. 'Thanks, John,' she said a trifle hoarsely. 'You've got a newcomer in the village. What do you think of her?'

'Mrs Fortune? Comes in here a lot. Nice lady. Very open-handed. Always buying drinks for everyone. She's the talk of the village. Bakes the best scones and cakes, best gardener, can do plumbing repairs, and knows all about car engines.'

Jimmy Page, one of the local farmers, came in and hailed Agatha. 'Right good to see you back, Agatha,' he said, hitching his large backside on to the bar stool next to her.

'What'll you have?' asked Agatha, determined not to be outdone in generosity by Mary.

'Half a pint,' said Jimmy.

'I've brought you and your wife a present,' said Agatha. 'I'll bring it along tomorrow.'

'Very good of you. No murders while you've been away. Quiet as the grave. That Mary Fortune, she said a funny thing. She says, "Maybe Mrs Raisin is like a sort of vulture, and as long as she's out of the village, nothing bad'll happen."'

'That wasn't a very nice thing to say.' Agatha glared.

'Don't you go taking it hard-like. Her's got this jokey way of saying things. Don't mean no harm. Tell me about your holiday.'

And as more locals came in to join them, Agatha elaborated on her adventures, inventing funny scenes and relishing being the centre of attention until a look at the clock behind the bar told her that she had better get along to the school hall.

In the dimness of the school hall and among what seemed to Agatha's jaundiced eyes to be the fustiest of the villagers, Mary with her blonde hair and green wool dress clinging to her excellent figure shone like the sun. She was sitting next to James, and as Agatha entered she heard Mary say, 'Perhaps we should have gone for dinner before this. I'm starving.'

So he had lied about getting something in for his supper, thought Agatha bleakly.

A Mr Bernard Spott, an elderly gentleman, led the meeting. There were familiar faces in the gloom of the school hall, where two fluorescent lights had failed to function and the remaining one whined and stuttered above their heads. Children's drawings were pinned up on the walls. There was something depressing about children's paintings on the walls of a room at an adult gathering, thought Agatha, as if underlining the fact that childhood was long gone and never to return. The Boggles were there, that sour elderly couple who complained about everything. Mrs Mason, who was chairwoman of the Carsely Ladies' Society, was in the front row beside Mrs Bloxby. Doris Simpson, Agatha's cleaner, came in and sat beside Agatha, muttering a 'Welcome back.' Behind her came Miss Simms, the unmarried mother who was secretary of the Ladies' Society, tottering on her high heels.

Mr Spott droned on about the annual horticultural show, which was to be held in July. After that, in August, there was the Great Day when the members of the society opened their gardens to the public. Fred Griggs, the local policeman, then read the minutes of the last meeting as if giving evidence in court.

Agatha stifled a yawn. What was the point of all this? James was definitely not interested in her and never would be. She regretted the expense of the greenhouse. She let her mind wander. It was surely wicked to wish for another murder, but that was what she found she was doing. She hated attending things like this where she knew she did not belong. Gardening, mused Agatha, was something one had to grow up doing. Any plant which had shown its head in the Birmingham slum in which she had been brought up had been promptly savaged by the local children.

There was a shuffling of feet as the meeting ended. And there was Mary, very much the hostess with the mostest, presiding over the tea-urn at the end of the hall.

Agatha turned to Doris. 'Thanks for keeping my place so clean,' she said. 'You into this gardening lark?'

'Just started last year,' said Doris. 'It's good fun.'

'This doesn't seem much like fun,' commented Agatha, looking sourly down the hall to where James was standing next to Mary, who was pouring tea and handing out plates of cakes.

'It gets better when things start growing.'

'Our newcomer appears highly popular,' said Agatha.

'Not with me.'

Oh, sensible Doris. Oh, treasure beyond compare! 'Why?'

'I dunno.' Doris's pale grey eyes were shrewd behind her glasses. 'She does everything right and she's right nice to everybody, but there's no warmth there. It's as if she's acting.'

'James Lacey seems taken with her.'

'That won't last.'

Agatha felt a sudden surge of hope. 'Why?'

'Because he's a clever man and she just appears clever. He's a nice man and she's only pretending to be nice. That's the way I see it.'

'I brought you a present,' said Agatha. 'You can collect it when you come round tomorrow.'

25

'Thanks a lot, but you shouldn't have bothered, really. How're your cats?'

'Ignoring me. Didn't like the cattery.'

'Instead of paying that cattery, next time you go off, leave them be and I'll come round every day and feed them and let them out for a bit. Better in their own home.'

Mrs Bloxby came up to them, followed by Miss Simms. She was wearing the new scarf. 'So pretty,' she said. 'I couldn't wait until Sunday to wear it.'

Agatha turned to Miss Simms. 'I have a present for you as well.'

'That's ever so nice of you,' said Miss Simms. 'But you haven't had any tea, Agatha, and Mary makes such good cakes.'

'Maybe next time,' replied Agatha, who had no intention of making herself suffer further by going and joining James and Mary.

Mary Fortune looked down the room at the ever growing group around Agatha Raisin. She began to pack up the tea things, putting the few cakes left in a plastic box.

'I'll carry that home for you,' said James. He could not help noticing as he left with Mary that the group about Agatha were laughing at something she was saying and no one turned to watch them go, but it would have amazed him to know that Agatha, although she never turned round, was aware, with every fibre of her being, of every step he took towards the door.

The night was crisp and cold and frosty. Great stars burnt overhead. James felt content with the world.

'That Agatha Raisin is a peculiarly vulgar type of woman,' he realized Mary was saying.

'Agatha can be a bit abrupt at times,' he said defensively, 'but she is actually very good-hearted.'

'Watch out, James,' teased Mary. 'Our repressed village spinster has her eye on you.'

'As far as I know, Agatha is a divorcée like yourself,' said James stiffly. Loyalty made him forget all the times he had avoided Agatha when she was pursuing him. 'I don't want to discuss her.'

She gave a little laugh. 'Poor James. Of course you don't.'

She began to talk about gardening and James walked beside her and tried to bring back the feelings of warmth and elation he usually felt in her company. But he had not liked her snide remark about Agatha. He admired bravery, and there was no doubt there was a certain gallantry about Agatha Raisin which appealed to him.

He saw Mary to her door and handed over the cake box, and to her obvious surprise refused her invitation for the usual cup of coffee.

*　　*　　*

Agatha, too preoccupied with the James-Mary business, had failed to notice her own popularity at the horticultural society. But Agatha had never been popular in her life before. She had been the successful owner of a public relations company, having only recently sold up and retired to move to Carsely. Hitherto, her work had been her life and her identity. The people in her life had been her staff, and the journalists whom she had bullied into giving space to whomever or whatever she happened to be promoting.

When she opened the door and the phone began to ring, she looked at it almost in surprise.

'Hello?' she asked tentatively.

'Aggie? How's life in Peasantville?' came the mincing tones of her ex-assistant, Roy Silver.

'Oh, Roy. How are you?' said Agatha.

'Working as usual, and feeling bored. Any hope of an invitation?'

Agatha hesitated. She wondered if she really liked Roy any more, or, for that matter, had ever liked him. She had invited him before when she was desperate for company. Still, it would be nice to talk PR for a change and find out what was going on in London.

'You can come this weekend,' she said. 'I'll pick you up in Moreton-in-Marsh. Got a girl?'

'No, just little me, sweetie. Still microwaving everything?'

28

'I'm a proper cook now,' said Agatha severely.

'I'll get the train that gets in about eleven thirty,' said Roy. 'See you then. Any murders?'

Agatha thought bitterly of Mary Fortune.

'Not yet,' she said. 'Not yet.'

Chapter Two

Agatha was surprised to receive a handwritten invitation to drinks at Mary's for Friday evening. It had been pushed through the letter-box the day after the horticultural society meeting.

She stared down at it as if it were some species of poisonous insect. She then walked up to her bedroom and surveyed herself in the mirror. Her figure had thickened with all the food she had eaten on her travels, comfort food to combat the loneliness. She looked decidedly matronly. She put the invitation down on the dressing-table and took one of her best dresses out of the wardrobe and, quickly slipping off the old sweater and trousers she was wearing, tried it on. To her relief it seemed to *look* the same, although it felt tight, but when she twisted round and surveyed her back, it was to see with dismay two rolls of fat above the line of her knickers. How could she go to Mary's and compete with her in any way? That was the trouble about being in one's fifties.

Unless one's figure was firmly kept in check at all times, it suddenly began to sag alarmingly and develop nasty rolls of fat.

She changed back and decided to put off accepting the invitation until she had thought clearly what to do. In the meanwhile, she would drive into one of the cheap supermarkets in Evesham and get food for the weekend, picking up some fresh fruit and vegetables from the open-air stands on the A44.

At the supermarket, she decided to have a cup of coffee in the café before shopping. She found that although she had brought cigarettes, she had left her lighter behind, so she went up to the cigarette counter and asked for a cheap lighter. 'These,' said the middle-aged assistant, 'are electronically controlled.'

'What does that mean?' asked Agatha.

'See, it clicks down without much pressure.' She beamed at Agatha. 'Very good for the elderly who have trouble with their thumbs.'

Agatha glared at her. 'I hate you.'

'Madam, I just said –'

'Never mind,' snarled Agatha, 'I'll take it. How much?'

'Eight-five pee. But –'

Agatha slammed down the right money, picked up the lighter and stormed off. Was this what happened at fifty-something when you didn't wear make-up? Getting mistaken for a geriatric?

Come on, sounded the voice of logic in her head, she didn't mean you. Oh, yes, she did, shrieked her bruised emotions. She got herself a cup of coffee at the self-service counter, winced away from the cream cakes and sat moodily down at the window and glared out at the car-park.

There is something very lowering about drinking coffee in a British supermarket while surveying the car-park. Trees surrounded it, wispy, newly planted trees which must have looked very neat and pretty when made out of green sponge on the architect's model. Agatha could almost imagine herself placed in the café window on the model, a small plastic Agatha. It was a dusty, windy day. Discarded wrappings spiralled up and a thin film of greasy rain began to blur the windows. Agatha sighed heavily. It would be very comfortable to forget about the James Laceys of this world and give up, become fat and contented, leave the skin creams alone and let the wrinkles happen. She would not go to Mary's. She would be sensible.

But there would be no harm in getting the bicycle out and taking some exercise.

Mary Fortune stood surveying her guests on Friday. She had a plentiful supply of drinks of all kinds and had cooked hot little savouries to go with them. But people weren't staying, and an awful lot of them had looked around and asked, 'Where's Mrs Raisin?' And Mary had replied sweetly that as Mrs Raisin was expecting a guest at the weekend, she was staying at home to make preparations. Jimmy Page, the farmer, said he thought he had seen Agatha heading for the Red Lion, and an irritating woman, Mrs Toms, said, 'Might just drop down there and thank her for that present,' and Mary began to feel that some of the departing guests were following suit. As a further irritation, James no longer looked at her with that glowing, shy sort of look but fidgeted about. Normally he would have kept at her side and then stayed behind to help her clear up. Mary was puzzled. From what she had seen of her, Agatha Raisin was a stocky, plain, middle-aged woman who had had a charm bypass, so James could not possibly have transferred his attentions to her. But it was almost as if this Agatha Raisin belonged to the villagers and the village, and she, Mary did not. And, sure enough, James did not stay.

Agatha waited the next morning at Moreton-in-Marsh station for the arrival of Roy Silver. She wished in a way he were not coming, perhaps because Roy with his waspish camp manner did not fit into the comfortable ways of Carsely. But

James Lacey could find nothing, well, romantic in the fact that Agatha had a man staying for the weekend. Roy was far too young, still in his twenties.

When Roy came sailing off the train dressed in black denim and talking into a mobile phone, Agatha's heart sank. Roy, satisfied at last that the few people on the station platform had noticed the young executive at work, rang off and approached Agatha.

'What have you been doing to yourself?' he asked by way of greeting. '"O, that this too, too solid flesh would melt . . ." Shakespeare, Aggie. Got a word for everything.'

'Taught you well in the reform school?' rejoined Agatha, who hated literary quotations.

'Honestly, darling,' went on Roy cheerfully, 'not like you to go to seed.'

'I put on a bit on my holidays,' said Agatha, 'but I'll soon take it off.'

'Go on a diet. I'll join you,' said Roy eagerly. 'The fruit diet's the thing. Eat nothing but fruit for three days, and I am here for three days.'

'Don't you have to be at work on Monday?'

'Got an extra day owing to me *and* I've got a proposition to put to you.'

'Oh, Roy, I didn't know you cared. Put that case of yours with the Costa del Sol labels in the back,' snapped Agatha, 'and let's get a move on.'

34

'Righty-ho. Tell you about it when we get to your place.'

Roy chattered along about the fruit diet, which he seemed determined they should both go on. Agatha drove steadily up through Bourton-on-the-Hill, noticing gloomily that there were still houses for sale, a sign that the recession was not disappearing as fast as the politicians wanted the public to think. She then turned down the long winding road which led to Carsely. There had been a heavy frost that morning, which had not yet melted. White trees leaned over the road and the whole countryside seemed still and frozen into immobility.

'Are you sure you want to go ahead with this diet?' she asked when she had ushered him into the cottage. 'I've got lots of goodies for the weekend, and I'm a fair cook.'

'Let's do it, Aggie. Just think how slim you'll look.'

And Agatha thought of Mary Fortune and heaved a little sigh. 'All right, Roy. Fruit it is.'

She said a longing mental goodbye to the lunch of grilled steak and baked potatoes she had planned. That wasn't fattening, she thought, forgetting about all the sour cream and fresh butter she was going to put on the potatoes.

'Like to go along to the pub for a drink?' she asked hopefully. On Saturdays the bar of the Red

Lion was covered in little dishes of cheese nibbles and pickled onions.

'Can't have alcohol or coffee,' said Roy cheerfully. 'We'd better go out and get some fruit.'

'I have fruit,' said Agatha, pointing to a full bowl of apples and oranges.'

'Not enough, sweetie. Must get more.'

As they approached her car parked outside in the lane, Agatha was tempted to tell Roy to forget about such a ridiculous diet. But Mary's car drew up outside James Lacey's and Mary got out wearing her favourite green. Mary cast a swift appraising look at Roy, and Agatha was suddenly conscious of Roy's youth and weediness. He had a thin white face and small clever eyes and a thin weedy body which looked as if it needed fattening up rather than dieting.

'Who's the glamour-puss?' asked Roy.

'Some incomer,' said Agatha sourly. 'Get in the car.'

Her stomach rumbled, reminding her that she had breakfasted on a cup of coffee and a cigarette.

But there was the carrot held out in front of her of an almost immediate loss of weight.

They drove to Evesham and bought apples, melons, bananas, grapes, pineapples, oranges and a selection of 'yuppie' fruit from an exotic and highly priced variety.

Back home again, they both ate as much as

they could and assured each other that they felt terribly well already. Then they went out cycling, Roy borrowing a cycle from the vicarage. It was to be the best part of the weekend as they flew along the frosty lanes in the clear air, returning home under a burning red sun which set the frost-covered grass and trees aflame and made the frozen puddles in the roads burn like monsters' eyes.

But instead of sitting down that evening to a warming meal, there was nothing but more fruit and mineral water.

'What's this proposition you were talking about?' asked Agatha.

'You remember Mr Wilson of Pedmans, my boss?'

Agatha's eyes narrowed. She had sold her PR business to Pedmans. Wilson had gone back on all his assurances that her offices and staff would remain intact, had fired the staff with the exception of Roy, and had sold the offices. 'Of course.'

'He was talking about you the other day. Said you were the best ever. I said I was going to see you,' said Roy, carefully and conveniently forgetting that his decision to visit Agatha had been prompted after he had heard his boss's praise of her. 'He said he would like to employ you as an executive. Pure Cosmetics are playing up. You used to handle them.'

'Bunch of toe-rags,' said Agatha moodily. Pure Cosmetics was run by a temperamental and demanding woman, a modern slave-driver.

'But that woman, Jessica Turnbull, the director of Pure Cosmetics, you could always handle her. That's what Wilson said.'

'I'm retired,' said Agatha. 'Hey, you're spotty.'

Roy squawked and ran upstairs to the bathroom. He returned and said, 'I look like a fourteen-year-old with acne. You're spotty as well.'

'Let's chuck this stupid diet.'

'No,' said Roy firmly. 'It's toxic waste. The impurities are being purged out of our bodies.'

'I agreed to this stupid thing to look better, not to get spotty.'

'But you look slimmer already, Aggie,' said Roy craftily. 'Don't think about Wilson's offer now. We'll watch that video I got and then we'll have an early night.'

Agatha awoke early the next day, hungry and bad-tempered. She went downstairs and gloomily ate six apples, drank a glass of mineral water, and smoked five cigarettes. The doorbell rang. She went to the door and peered through the spyhole. She recognized James Lacey's chest, which was all she could see of him.

She put her hands up to her face. She could almost feel the spots.

38

Agatha backed away from the door. She longed to open it, but not like this, not spotty-faced and in her dressing gown.

Outside, James turned slowly away. He had just decided it was silly to nourish a childish resentment of Agatha because she had made a rude gesture at him, and all that time ago, too. As he approached his cottage, he saw Mary's blonde head turning into the lane. Without thinking why, he quickened his step and plunged into his cottage like some large animal into its burrow, and when his own doorbell rang imperatively a few moments later, he did not answer it, persuading himself that he needed to get down to work.

He was still working on a history of the Peninsular Wars. He switched on his computer and looked gloomily at the last paragraph he'd written. Then he flicked it off and stared moodily at the screen. There was a heading saying simply, 'Case'. That was when Agatha and he had been trying to solve a murder and he had typed out all the facts and had studied them. That had been fun. It had been exciting. Perhaps Agatha was on to something new. He shook his head. No one had been murdered for miles around. Carsely was still locked in its winter's sleep. He wondered uneasily why Agatha had not answered the door. She must have been home because her car was parked outside and smoke had been rising from the chimney. That fellow Roy was staying with her. He had seen them the day before on their bicycles. There couldn't be any romantic interest there. The fellow was too young. Still, in these modern days of toy boys, one could never tell. They were probably having a high old time, laughing and joking while he sat sunk in boredom.

'I don't like Wilson and I don't like Pedmans,' Agatha was saying sourly. 'I loathe fruit and I could kill for a big greasy hamburger.'

'Take a look in the mirror,' retorted Roy crossly, made bitter by diet and the fact that his mission was to get Agatha back to work. 'You've let yourself go. Okay, so you've had a bit of excitement in this place before, but nothing is ever going to happen here again and you may as well make up your mind to it. Think of London, Aggie!'

And Agatha thought of London and thought of how odd and alien she felt now on her infrequent visits – London, which had once been the centre of her universe.

'I'm happy here,' she said defiantly. 'All right, I've let myself go a tiny bit, but I'll be back on form soon enough.'

'But Wilson's prepared to offer you eighty-five thousand a year, for starters.'

Agatha's eyes narrowed. 'Wait a bit. You and

Wilson seem to have discussed this thoroughly, and knowing what a weak little creep you are, Roy, you probably said, "Leave it to me. I'll nip down there for the weekend and get the old girl to come around." You probably bragged as well. "Oh, Aggie and I are like *that*. She'd do anything for me."'

This was so nearly exactly what Roy had said that he blushed under his spots and then became furious. 'No, it's not at all what happened,' he screeched. 'The trouble with you, Aggie, is that you wouldn't know a real friend if you met one in your soup. I'm sick of this, sick of this. I'm going up to shave and get packed.'

'Do that,' Agatha shouted after him, 'but watch your spots. In fact, to help you on your way, I'll run you into Oxford!'

An hour later, they set off together on the Oxford road, Agatha driving in a bitter silence. Her stomach wasn't rumbling, it was letting out moans. She hated Roy, she hated Carsely, she hated James Lacey, she hated the whole of the Carsely Ladies' Society, she hated Mrs Bloxby . . .

She was driving along the A40 as that last name in the catalogue came into her mind. She swerved off the road and parked outside a restaurant.

'So what are we doing here?' demanded Roy,

speaking for the first time since they had left the village.

'I don't know about you, but I am going to eat one great big hamburger smothered in ketchup,' said Agatha. 'You can watch me or join me, I don't care.'

Roy followed her into the restaurant and then watched moodily as she ordered coffee and a 'giant' hamburger and 'giant' French fries. Then, in a tight, squeaky voice, he said to the waitress, 'The same for me.'

When the food arrived, they ate their way stolidly through it. Then Agatha imperiously summoned the waitress. 'Same again,' she said.

'Same again,' said Roy, through a sudden fit of the giggles.

'Sorry I was so bitchy,' said Agatha. 'Can't stand diets.'

'That's all right, Aggie,' said Roy. 'Can be a bit of a bitch myself.'

'And thank Wilson for his offer and tell him I'll think about it. And –' Agatha leaned back and dabbed at her greasy mouth and gave a small burp – 'tell him I would do it for you if I did it for anyone.'

'Thanks, Aggie.'

'Furthermore, I'll run you all the way to London if you'll join me in ordering a large amount of chocolate cake with chocolate sauce and ice cream.'

'You're on.'

When they left the diner they were laughing and giggling as if they had been drinking instead of eating. They sang all the way to London and told jokes until Agatha dropped Roy outside his Chelsea flat.

'Why not stay the night?' said Roy.

'No, I've got my cats to feed. Must get home.'

'Well, your spots have gone.'

'So they have.' Agatha peered in the driving mirror. 'Nothing's better for the skin than a greasy hamburger.'

She felt quite happy when she reached Carsely again. She would attend the Carsely Ladies' Society meeting that evening at the vicarage. When she walked into the kitchen and saw bowls piled high with fruit, she gave a shudder. There would be sandwiches and fruit cake and perhaps one of Miss Simms's chocolate cakes and she intended to eat as much as she could. Her figure could wait.

It was only when she was seated in the vicarage and reaching out for the first ham sandwich that she realized she had felt no desire to stay in London. Her cleaner had the key to the cottage and would gladly have fed the cats if Agatha had decided to stay in town for the night. Changed days, thought Agatha, where tea and sandwiches at the vicarage took precedence over anything London had to offer.

And then Mary Fortune walked into the room, borne forward on a cloud of French perfume. She was slim but curvaceous in tailored trousers, silk blouse and jacket. All green. She never seemed to wear any other colour.

Agatha, her mouth full of sandwich, was dismally aware of the tightness of the skirt she was wearing. As she looked at Mary, she felt herself becoming fatter and fatter. Mary was carrying a cake she had baked and the women were exclaiming in delight. Caraway cake! How clever! Thought no one still remembered how to bake one. Mary beamed all round as she accepted their plaudits. She saw an empty seat next to Agatha and came and sat down next to her.

'I'm glad you are joining the horticultural society,' said Mary with a charming smile.

'I've ordered a greenhouse,' said Agatha. 'Going to plant my own stuff this year.'

'I'll be glad to give you any cuttings you want,' said Mary.

Reflecting that she wouldn't have the faintest idea what to do with a cutting, Agatha mumbled thanks. Mary was obviously making a determined effort to please, and something in the new Agatha Raisin that was capable of reaching out to any offered warmth like a frost-bitten plant towards the sun, responded gradually with equal warmth. Agatha found herself inviting Mary round for coffee the following morning.

The meeting started with a discussion on catering. Soon after the annual horticultural show, the gardens of Carsely were open to the public to raise money for charity. The Ladies' Society had been approached by the horticultural society, who wanted them to serve teas in the school hall. Agatha, who usually liked to be at the centre of things, kept her mouth shut. She decided at that moment that all her energies must be conserved for *her* garden. People would flock to see it and it would glow with colour and outshine James Lacey's next door. In fact, it would outshine every other garden in the village. She could almost see James's face glowing with admiration.

The next morning, Agatha remembered her invitation to Mary. She decided not to bother dressing up. She put on a comfortable but baggy skirt with a loose blouse over it.

But the minute Mary arrived, Agatha wished she had put in some work on her appearance. Mary was wearing a green wool dress which clung to her figure, a figure which had bumps only in the right places. Over it she wore a loose coat of greenish tweed, and despite the coldness of the day outside, Mary was wearing very high-heeled green leather sandals and sheer stockings.

Mary slung off her coat, which she had been wearing loose around her shoulders, and dropped it on a chair. 'What a charming place you have, Mrs Raisin,' she said, looking around. 'I am glad of this opportunity to get to know each other better. Carsely is very pleasant, but people here do not travel much. In fact, for most of them a trip to the market in Moreton is a great adventure.'

'I believe you spent some time in America,' said Agatha, for the first time not wanting to be classed as different from the other village women.

'Yes, New York.'

Agatha had a vague idea that California was the home of the face-lift but decided that they probably had plenty of cosmetic surgeons in New York. There was a plastic look about Mary's face. Still, it could be her, Agatha's, jealousy prompting her to believe it was the result of a face-lift.

'I'll just get the coffee,' said Agatha and then her doorbell rang.

She went and opened it and found James Lacey standing on the step. Her first thought was that he had seen Mary going into her house and that was the reason for the call. 'Come in,' she said bleakly, 'Mary's here,' and turned away immediately and so missed the slightly hunted look in his eyes. In the kitchen, Agatha piled coffee-cups and warmed-up Danish pastries, plates and napkins on to a tray and decided to give up on James Lacey entirely. But she still had a nagging longing to escape upstairs and put on something more glamorous.

James looked up as Agatha came into the room and courteously rose to his feet and took the tray from her and set it on the table. For some reason there was an awkward silence. Agatha wondered what they had been talking about in the brief time she had been out of the room. The fire crackled, the china clinked as she arranged spoons on saucers, and from outside a starling gave out the long descending, sorrowful note of winter.

'I can't stay very long,' said James. 'Just dropped by to see how you were.'

'My morning for callers,' said Agatha as the doorbell went again.

When she opened it, she saw with surprise and delight that her visitor was Detective Sergeant Bill Wong. 'Heard through the grapevine you were back,' he said cheerfully. 'May I come in?'

'Of course,' said Agatha, longing to give the young man a hug but feeling uncharacteristically shy. 'I've got James here and a newcomer, Mary Fortune.'

Mary looked up as Bill Wong came in. She saw a small, chubby man with an oriental cast of features and very shrewd eyes.

Agatha went to get another cup and Bill followed her into the kitchen. 'Competition, Agatha?' he asked gently.

They had come to know each other very well during what Agatha thought of as her 'cases', but she felt that last remark had been going too far.

'I don't know what you mean,' she said huffily.

'Oh, yes, you do,' said Bill, taking a cup from her. 'You'll be getting a face-lift yourself soon.'

Agatha grinned at him. 'And I'd nearly forgotten how much I like you.'

Somehow Bill's very presence made her face Mary and James with equanimity. She introduced Bill properly to Mary and then asked him eagerly about what he was working on.

'The usual round of things,' said Bill. 'You haven't been around for a while, Agatha, so no one has been getting themselves murdered. But there have been terrible amounts of burglaries in the villages. They come down the motorways from Birmingham and London, finding the villages an easy target because people here don't go in so much for security and burglar alarms, and a lot of them still leave their cars unlocked and their doors open. You're well protected here,

Agatha. Very sensible of you to get that alarm system in.'

'Perhaps we should all follow Agatha's example,' said James.

Mary gave a little laugh. 'Some of us are not made of money. I think I will continue to trust human nature.'

'I don't think Agatha here is made of money either,' said Bill sharply, 'and considering the reason that she got the system in was because her life was under threat, I think that remark of yours was uncalled for.'

It was obvious to James that Mary was not used to being pulled up for one of her 'little remarks'. Then he realized with surprise that Mary quite often said things which could easily be classed as bitchy. He began to feel he had made a bit of a fool of himself over Mary.

Mary turned slightly pink and said quickly, 'I didn't mean *Agatha*. How could you think such a thing! You didn't think I meant you, did you, Agatha?'

'Yes, I did,' said Agatha.

Mary spread her well-manicured hands in a deprecatory gesture. 'What more can I say? I'm sorry, sorry, *sorry*.'

'You're forgiven,' said Agatha gruffly.

'When is your greenhouse arriving?' asked Mary.

'Today. Any minute now.'

Bill's narrow eyes filled with humour as he looked at Agatha. 'Never tell me you're going in for serious gardening?'

'Might try my hand. I've joined the horticultural society.'

Bill raised his hands in mock horror. 'Don't tell me someone is going to be murdered. Don't tell me you will be going in for any competitions.'

'Why not?' asked Mary in surprise. 'That's part of the fun. We have the annual show and it's a very friendly affair, I gather.'

'You haven't had Agatha in the society before,' said Bill.

'How's your book coming along?' Agatha had turned to James, feeling that if Bill went on he might reveal how she had once cheated in the village baking competition.

'Slowly,' said James. 'I try to knuckle down to it and all the while I'm praying for the phone to ring or someone to call to distract me. Are you going to use the greenhouse right away, Agatha?'

'Yes, I'm going to get some seed boxes and plant some things.'

'Tell you what,' said James, 'I'll go to the nursery with you and help you to choose something.'

Agatha brightened but Mary said, 'We'll *all* go.'

'Let me know, anyway.' James got to his feet.

'I'd best be going as well.' Mary picked up her coat. 'Lovely coffee. Probably see you later at the Red Lion. Come along, James.'

James immediately felt like sitting down again, but he went off with Mary. Agatha slammed the door behind them with unnecessary force and went back to join Bill.

'Handsome couple,' commented Bill maliciously.

'Drink your coffee,' said Agatha sourly.

'I'm teasing you. He actually doesn't like her.'

'But I gather they've been an item!'

'They might have been. But not any more. Take things easy, Agatha. Relax. If you behave in a quiet, friendly way to him, he'll come around.'

'I've decided I'm not interested any more. I mean, if he fancied someone like Mary Fortune, I don't think I want to know.'

Bill shook his head. 'You don't know much about him. There's your doorbell again.'

Agatha ran to the door. Perhaps he had come back. But it was the men with the greenhouse.

Bill took his leave with promises to return and left Agatha with the workmen.

By the end of that day a small new greenhouse glittered at the end of Agatha's garden. She restrained an impulse to rush next door to ask James to come with her to a nursery the following day. He might just remind her that Mary wanted to come along as well.

So instead she went to the Red Lion. It was one of these odd evenings when the pub was thin of company. She talked to a few of the locals, her eyes always straying to the door, waiting for the tall figure of James Lacey to appear.

She made her way home finally, slightly tipsy, and went disconsolately to bed.

The following day she felt bloated, old and downright plain. She sadly took herself off to a local nursery to ask their advice and returned home with packets of seeds, seed trays and instructions which she had written down. She worked busily, planting trays of chrysanthemum, Coltness Mixture and Rigoletto. Then she planted trays of *Arctotis hybrida*, or African daisy. By evening she had finished her work with trays of hibiscus, a variety called Disco Belle. The hibiscus and the chrysanthemums were supposed to be sown in February and planted out in May, but she had been told to sow the African daisies in March. But, thought Agatha, the work was so soothing and it was nearly the end of February anyway. All of them would then be planted out in May.

Next door, James could see Agatha bent over her work in the greenhouse. He felt disappointed that she had not asked for his help.

Chapter Three

As a reluctant spring crept over the Cotswolds, Agatha's mind often turned to Wilson's offer of a job. At last he phoned her himself and she told him that she might be ready to start work in the autumn, because by the autumn the gardening days would be over. Mary had become a friend, despite Agatha's initial reluctance. She was always charming, always ready to help, and her close relationship with James Lacey appeared to be at an end.

Daffodils shone in the gardens of the village, and then came the cascades of wisteria and heavy lilac blossoms. It was such a miserable spring that it seemed incredible that anything could blossom at all in the slashing rain and gusts of chilly wind. Agatha intended to plant out her seedlings on the first of May. She had bought more trays of seedlings from the nursery and they lay alongside the 'home-grown' products in her greenhouse waiting for the big day.

She had promised Mrs Bloxby to help at the tombola stand on May Monday, which was when all the village celebrations were to take place. Sunday was to be May the first.

It was on Friday, the twenty-ninth of April, that James decided he had been too hard on Agatha. She had in the past made him countless cups of coffee and brought him cakes. They had shared many adventures together. It nagged at his mind that he had taken Mary Fortune out for several dinners while Agatha had been away, and yet he had never asked Agatha out. He had at one time, he admitted, thought that Agatha was keen on him and he had shied away from the thought. But the woman had been all that was normal. In fact, she had never called on him.

So on Friday morning he went and rang her doorbell and asked a flustered Agatha – flustered because she was still in her dressing-gown – out to dinner at a new restaurant in Moreton, the Game Bird.

Gardening forgotten for once, Agatha passed the day in a daze of preparation, finding to her delight that gardening, along with a moderate diet, definitely had its compensations, for all her dresses now fitted her beautifully. She winced at the sight of a green dress. Definitely not green. Mary never wore anything else. She wondered vaguely about the mentality of a woman who always wore one colour. She took herself off to Oxford and got her hair cut and shaped. She bought new cosmetics. She bought new high heels and then, when she returned from Oxford, realized she had only left herself an hour to get ready, and she had originally planned to take two hours beautifying herself.

The doorbell rang just as she had finished. Thinking James was ten minutes early, she went to answer it. Mary stood there wearing the inevitable green; green blouse, green jacket, green slacks, green leather high-heeled sandals. She blinked a little at the sight of the new Agatha Raisin in little black dress, gold jewellery, and with her short brown hair gleaming in the light over the door.

'Coming to the pub?' asked Mary.

'Can't,' said Agatha cheerfully. 'James is taking me out for dinner.'

Mary's blue eyes went quite blank and then she said with a little laugh. 'Tomorrow then?'

'I'll meet you there at seven,' said Agatha. Mary waited, but no, Agatha was not going to spoil this golden meeting by inviting Mary in and risking having Mary include herself in the invitation when James arrived. 'See you,' said Agatha brightly and slammed the door.

She then waited in the hall in a frenzy of impatience. What if Mary should now call on James? What if they both came back together?

What if James said, 'Mary's going to join us'? What if . . .?

The doorbell rang, making her jump. Crossing the fingers of one hand, she opened the door with the other and let out a sigh of relief to see James there on his own, wearing a well-cut dark suit and looking heart-wrenchingly handsome.

'Whose car are we taking?' asked Agatha. 'Which one of us is going to do without drink?'

'Neither,' he said with a smile. He looked down the lane. 'Our taxi is just arriving.'

Agatha, made shy by happiness, sat very upright in the back seat of the taxi with James. Mrs Mason stopped on the corner and looked curiously at them as she passed and then made her way to the Red Lion. By midnight, there would be very few people in Carsely who did not know that James Lacey had driven off with Agatha Raisin in a taxi.

Agatha, although she was slowly coming to appreciate good food and yet still was quite happy with junk, nonetheless had a sharp eye for a rip-off and her heart sank a little as they entered the elegant country-house atmosphere of the Game Bird. And yet all was calm and soothing. They had a drink in the small bar, seated in chintz-covered armchairs before a roaring log fire. Perhaps, thought Agatha, it was because the tablecloths in the dining-room were pink, as were the napkins. There was always something suspicious about restaurants which went in for pink tablecloths.

When they sat down at the table, huge menus were handed to them, the kind that are handwritten as if by a doctor, the writing is so nearly indecipherable.

It was very expensive and she blinked at the prices. But she was very hungry after her weeks of dieting and gardening – no fruit diet, just eating less – and decided to splash out. She ordered bouillabaisse, followed by the 'venison special', despite James's murmur that April might not be a good time to order venison.

'You forget,' said Agatha, 'that there is a lot of farm venison around these days.'

They talked about people in the village and James said he, too, would be planting out his seedlings. The bouillabaisse arrived. But it was nothing more than a rather thin fish bisque – no bits of seafood – and served only with one sliver of toast melba, and the soup was served in a very small bowl.

James had a tiny portion of pâté, which was beautifully arranged on a small plate.

Determined to be good and not to make a fuss, Agatha drank her soup. She was still hungry when she had finished but then there was the venison to look forward to. The wine, although French vintage, and claiming to be Montrechat, tasted even to Agatha's untutored palate thin and vinegary.

But then her venison arrived. It was a small piece surrounded by carefully sculptured vegetables and covered in a cranberry sauce. No vulgar fattening potatoes. 'That looks good,' said James heartily, a shade too heartily. He had ordered duck in orange sauce.

Agatha attacked her venison. One cut, one mouthful proved her worst fears. Never had she seen a piece of meat with so much gristle. Her stomach let out a baffled rumble of disappointment.

She cracked.

Agatha imperiously summoned the head waiter. 'Yes, madam?' He stooped over the table.

'Can you tell me,' said Agatha in a thin voice, 'which part of the animal this comes from? Its hooves? Its knees? The bit between its eyes?'

'Perhaps madam is not accustomed to venison?'

Deep down inside her, Agatha's working-class soul flinched. Her temper snapped. 'Don't you dare patronize me,' she said. 'This is a lump of gristle. And while we're on the subject, that bouillabaisse was a rip-off, too.'

'Dear me,' said an acidulous-looking woman with a strangled would-be upper-class voice from the table behind Agatha, 'the tourist season is here again.'

Agatha whipped round. 'Screw you,' she said contemptuously. Then she turned her bearlike eyes back to the head waiter. 'I'm telling you this stuff is crap.'

Her voice had been overloud. Everyone had stopped talking and was staring at her. She flushed red.

'I don't know about the venison,' said James mildly, 'but this duck is as tough as old boots and appears to have been microwaved.'

'I will get the owner,' intoned the head waiter.

'I'm sorry, James,' said Agatha miserably.

He leaned across the table and poked at Agatha's venison experimentally with his fork. 'You know, you're right,' he said. 'It is a lump of gristle. And here, unless I am mistaken, comes the owner.'

A huge man bore down on their table. He had a large body and a surprisingly small head. 'I know your sort,' he said in a thick Italian accent. 'Get outta here. You don't wanna pay. So don't pay.'

'We do not mind paying,' said James stiffly, 'just so long as you take this away and bring us some decent food.'

The owner let out a growl of rage like a Klingon at a death ritual and seized the four corners of the tablecloth. He gathered up the lot and strode off to the kitchen with it over his shoulder, wine and gravy dripping down his massive back.

'Time to leave,' said James. He stood up and helped Agatha out of her chair.

Covered in shame, Agatha went outside. It was a clear, starry night. Far above the Fosse they twinkled, cold and remote from the social anguish of one middle-aged lady who felt she had not only blown the evening but destroyed all her hopes of romance. And then she realized James was laughing. He was leaning against the wall of the restaurant, laughing and laughing. At last he looked down at her, his eyes glinting in the streetlights. 'Oh, Agatha Raisin,' he said, 'I do love you when you're angry.'

And suddenly the stars above whirled and the Fosse became a Parisian boulevard and the world was young again and Agatha Raisin was young and pretty and attractive.

She grinned and said, 'Let's go to the pub next door and get some beer and sandwiches.'

Most of the pubs in the Cotswolds are comfortable places, redolent of age and centuries of good living. The sandwiches were delicious and the beer was good. They talked comfortably like old friends, Agatha cautiously determined to be on her best behaviour.

'We must do this again,' he said after he had

called for a taxi to take them home. 'A very cheap evening after all.'

And Agatha, a few minutes later sitting beside him in the taxi, reflected that if one is in the grip of an obsession, nothing is ever enough. She had told herself at the beginning of the evening that all she wanted was for them to be friends again, but now she longed for him to put an arm around her shoulders in the darkness of the taxi and kiss her. The longing was so intense that she felt her breathing becoming ragged and was half sad, half relieved when the short journey was over and he refused her offer of coffee, but said he would no doubt see her in the pub on the following day.

Agatha's heart sang as she went to bed. She fell asleep remembering every word and every look.

A visit from Mrs Mason the following day brought her down to earth. 'I saw you driving off with Mr Lacey in a taxi,' said Mrs Mason, settling her large bottom more comfortably in one of Agatha's armchairs.

'Yes, we had a nice evening,' said Agatha.

'Where did you go?'

'That new restaurant in Moreton, the Game Bird.'

'He entertains well when he takes the ladies

out,' said Mrs Mason. 'I've heard it's expensive.'

'What do you mean, he entertains well?'

'I know he took Mrs Fortune to the Lygon in Broadway at least a couple of times and once to the Randolph in Oxford.'

Agatha felt bleak. What was one disastrous dinner compared to what appeared to be a chain of good and expensive dinners he had enjoyed with Mary Fortune? She imagined them together on a long drive to Oxford. All the glory of the previous evening was tarnished. Agatha also found to her surprise that she actually liked Mary. Mary had become a good friend. Perhaps the most graceful thing to do would be to give up trying. On the other hand, James had shown no particular interest in Mary of late.

With only half her mind on what Mrs Mason was saying, Mrs Mason having gone on to talk about parish matters, Agatha wrestled with the problem of whether to go to the Red Lion that evening or not. Perhaps she should give up this village life and return to work in London. She still had not said no to Wilson's offer. He had phoned her again and been most persuasive. But, she thought, looking at the motherly bulk of Mrs Mason, friends had not dropped round to her flat for a chat in London. In fact, she had had no friends at all.

After Mrs Mason left, she went out into her

garden, which was cleared and ready for planting. It was a balmy day with big castles of white clouds floating over the Cotswold hills. Yes, she would go to the pub, but not to see James Lacey, just to meet people and have a chat.

But that evening she dressed with special care. She did not want to look *too* dressed up for a village pub and at last settled on a soft silk chiffon blouse of deep red worn with a short straight black skirt and black suede shoes with a modest heel. She gave herself a temporary face-lift with white of egg, very effective provided one did not smile too much, and strolled off in the direction of the pub. James's house had an empty look. He must be already there. With a feeling of going on-stage, she opened the pub door and went into the smoky low-ceilinged room. James was standing at the bar talking to Mr Bernard Spott, the man who headed the horticultural society. James hailed Agatha and bought her a gin and tonic. She had just taken her first sip and was looking for an inroad into the conversation about dahlias that James was having with Bernard when the pub door opened and Mary Fortune sailed in. Agatha had known the pangs of jealousy before but never anything as bad as this. She felt her face becoming stiff, as stiff as if she had just applied the white of egg.

Mary was wearing a short white jersey dress

and gold jewellery. The dress clung to her excellent figure. It was the first time Agatha had seen her wear anything other than green. The skirt of the dress was very short, exposing Mary's long legs encased in tan stockings and ending in high-heeled strapped sandals. Her golden hair glowed in the light. Her eyes were very wide and very blue. She had never looked more magnificent and her entrance was greeted with a sudden appreciative silence. James, too, had fallen silent and was gazing at Mary in open admiration. Oh, jealousy as sour as bile engulfed Agatha. She felt old and diminished.

James found his voice. 'Mary,' he said warmly. 'What are you having?'

'Campari soda, darling.' Mary linked her hand over his arm and smiled at him in an intimate way that made Agatha want to strike her. Old Bernard was tugging at his tie and staring at her in rapture. 'What were you talking about?' asked Mary.

'Gardening,' said James.

'Tomorrow's my big day,' declared Agatha. 'I'm planting out my seedlings.'

'Oh, I wouldn't do that, Agatha,' exclaimed Mary. 'There's going to be a big frost on Sunday night. I'm leaving mine until the weather settles.'

Was it Agatha's soured imagination, or was

this delivered with a certain, well, patronizing air?

'I didn't hear anything about frost,' she said mulishly.

Bernard Spott was a tall, thin man in his eighties, whose sparse grey hair was greased in strips over his scalp. He had a large beaky nose with which he looked down at whomever he was speaking to. He waggled an admonitory finger under Agatha's nose. 'Better listen to what Mary says. She's our expert.'

'Certainly is,' murmured James.

Agatha gave what she hoped was an enigmatic smile. The evening then proceeded to be a total disaster for her. If one has never had anything to do with gardening before, then one has little to contribute to a conversation in which a bewildering set of Latin names fly back and forth. And so Agatha stood mostly silent, as the names came and went and mulch was discussed and other organic fertilizers. Mary held court and Agatha stood on the outskirts. At last, when she saw her cleaner, Doris Simpson, and her husband seated over in a corner of the bar, Agatha murmured an excuse and went to join them.

Doris did not help Agatha's burning jealousy by remarking, 'Mrs Fortune looks like one of them film stars tonight.'

Agatha turned the conversation away from

Mary but all the while she talked of village matters she had half an ear tuned to the sound of James's frequent bursts of laughter.

Suddenly she couldn't bear it any more. She rose, said, 'Goodnight,' abruptly, and walked straight out of the pub, looking neither to right nor left.

Doris looked at her husband, her eyes shrewd behind her spectacles. 'The next murder done in this village,' she said, 'will be committed by our Agatha.'

Agatha stared up at the calm starlit sky as she walked home. The night air was balmy against her cheek. Frost, indeed. She was going to plant out her seedlings tomorrow and nothing was going to stop her!

The next day was sunny and warm, warm enough to wear a short-sleeved blouse, and Agatha hummed to herself as she planted out those tender green seedlings in well-weeded flowerbeds. She felt quiet and content. She felt she was getting on top of this gardening thing. That was the trouble about gardeners, they like to blast you with science, when it was all quite easy, really.

Before the light faded, she took a last look around the garden. She shivered in the sudden chill as the large red sun sank down behind the Cotswold hills. She glared up at the sky. There couldn't be frost, could there? Agatha, like most of the British public, swore that the meteorologists were often wrong, forgetting all the times they were right.

She stood there until the sun had disappeared, taking the light from the garden, bleaching the green from the plants. It was all so very still and quiet. A dog barked somewhere up on the fields above, its sudden noise intensifying the silence that followed.

Agatha shook her head like a baffled bull. It was nearly summer. By frost they had meant a little nip in the air, not that nasty white stuff which blanketed the Cotswolds in winter.

She went indoors, determined to watch some television and have an early night. She would set the alarm for six in the morning and would no doubt awake to a warm day.

When the alarm went off at six, shrill and imperative, she looked at it blearily, her first thought being that she had to get to the airport, which had been the case the last time she had set the alarm for six. Then memory came back. She threw back the duvet, went to the window, which overlooked the garden, took a deep breath and pulled back the curtains.

White! Everywhere. Thick white frost under

the pale dawn sky. Her eyes fell slowly to the plants. Surely they would have survived. She would not fret. She would get back into bed and wait for the sun to rise and then everything would be all right. And, despite her worry, she did fall asleep and did not awake until nine. She determinedly avoided looking out of the window. She showered and dressed in the old skirt and blouse she used for gardening and then she went downstairs and marched out into the garden. The sun was blazing, the frost was melting, and it was melting to reveal each pathetic little shrivelled and blackened plant that she had so lovingly placed in the earth the day before.

She wanted someone to turn to for help. But who? She didn't want her failure spread all over the village. James certainly wouldn't tell anyone but he would tell her she ought to have listened to Mary, and Agatha felt she couldn't bear that.

And then she thought of Roy Silver. She went indoors and rang his London number.

Roy was off work because it was a bank holiday. He complained Agatha's call had dragged him out of bed.

'Listen,' snapped Agatha, cutting across his complaints. She told him about the frost and how she had refused to take advice. 'And now,' she wailed, 'I'll be damned as a failed gardener.'

'No, no, no, sweetie. It's no use going on like

a sandwich short of a picnic. Cunning is what you need here. Low cunning. You've got used to simple village ways. Let me think. You know that nursery chain I handle?'

'Yes, yes. But I'm surrounded with nurseries down here.'

'Listen. Keep everyone out of your garden. Can that Lacey chap see into it from next door?'

'There's a hedge between us. He would need to hang out of the window and crane his neck.'

'Good. Now that account Wilson wants you to handle. If I can get you to promise you'll give him six months of your time, say, starting in September, I'll be down there with a truck of super-duper fencing.'

'I've got fencing!'

'You want the high non-see-through type. I'll come with workmen. We'll put it up all round the garden, and don't let anyone out the back. Then, before the big day, I'll come down with a load of fully grown exotica, stuff it in the good earth, and bingo! You'll be the talk of the village.'

'But what about Doris, my cleaner? She'll find out.'

'Swear her to secrecy, but no one else.'

'I could do it,' said Agatha doubtfully, 'but six months working for Wilson . . .'

'Do it. What's six months?'

A lot when you get to my age, thought Agatha sadly after she had agreed to his plan and put down the phone.

She could not help feeling like a criminal. What did it all matter anyway? But she did so hope to score over Mary.

A ring at her doorbell made her jump guiltily. She opened it cautiously and saw Mrs Bloxby.

'Did you sleep in?' asked the vicar's wife anxiously.

'No,' said Agatha. 'What's the matter?'

'You're supposed to be manning the tombola stand. Is one allowed to say "manning" these days? Does one say womaning or personing? Anyway, Mrs Mason and I have it all set up.'

'Oh.' Agatha blushed guiltily. 'I had forgotten. I've got some men coming to put in new fencing.'

Mrs Bloxby looked surprised. 'As I remember, there is a very good strong pine fence around your garden.'

'Falling apart in bits,' lied Agatha. She thought quickly. She could leave a note on the door for Roy saying she was at the tombola stand, and when he came along she could give him the keys. Not that he really needed them. The workmen could get to the back garden along the path at the side of the house.

'Give me five minutes,' she said. 'I'll follow you along.'

She wrote a note for Roy and pinned it to the door. The May festivities would take all day. On the other hand, if she could do a good sales pitch at the tombola stand, perhaps she could clear it quickly and then she would be free.

The one good thing, she thought as she made her way to the fair, which was taking up the length of the main street, blocked off to traffic for the day, was that practically everyone at the village would be working at or watching the festivities, and so there would be no one around to ask awkward questions about the fencing.

She took her place behind the table, which held a motley collection of prizes. Apart from a bottle of whisky and a bottle of wine presented by the Red Lion, the rest were odds and ends, a can of pilchards, for example, and a bottle of shampoo 'for brunettes'.

Most of the crowd of locals and tourists were watching the schoolchildren dancing around the maypole. Agatha fretted until the dancing ended in the crowning of the May Queen, a little girl with a sweet old-fashioned face, and then she gave tongue. 'Roll up! Roll up!' she shouted. 'Loads of prizes to be won. Tickets only twenty pee.'

Startled and then amused at such hustling in a quiet village, people began to gather round.

Agatha had quickly slipped the tickets for the bottle of wine and the bottle of whisky into her pocket. She knew the sight of them, unwon, would spur the punters on.

'Oh, you've won the can of pilchards,' she said to elderly Mrs Boggle.

'So what?' grumbled Mrs Boggle. 'I wanted the Scotch.'

'Lovely for sandwiches, those pilchards,' said Agatha cheerfully. 'Try again.'

So Mrs Boggle reluctantly prised a twenty-pence piece out of an ancient purse and handed it over. She won again, this time the shampoo for brunettes. 'This is a rip-off,' said Mrs Boggle. 'I'm grey-haired.'

'Then that'll turn you brown and make you look years younger,' snapped Agatha. 'Next!'

Mrs Boggle shuffled off. Agatha's voice rose in pitch. 'Roll up! Roll up! What have we here? A set of plastic egg-cups. Very useful. Come along. All in a good cause.'

'Does she usually go on like that?' Mary Fortune, over at the home-made cake stall, asked Mrs Bloxby.

'Mrs Raisin is an excellent saleswoman,' said Mrs Bloxby, 'and uses her talents to help the village.'

Despite Agatha's efforts, the day crawled on. Just as she got a crowd of people around the tombola stand, another diversion, such as dancing by the morris men, would take them all away again.

It was late afternoon when Roy popped up at Agatha's elbow. 'You'd better come home,' he said. 'I've got the workmen there and they need to put a padlocked gate on that path to the back garden. See, I thought of everything. And the fencing is sectioned. On the big day they'll take the top section off.'

'Oh, Roy, look, I'll give you the keys. Go along and take care of everything. I can't move until I've shifted this lot.'

'No, you've got to be there yourself.'

'Here . . .' Agatha slipped him a twenty-pound note. 'Buy all the tickets and let me out of here.'

She quickly slipped the tickets for the whisky and the wine back into the box.

'Damn, I have to open all these,' grumbled Roy, opening ticket after ticket. 'Really, Aggie, plastic egg-cups, a tea-cosy, and a scarf in magenta and sulphur-yellow.'

Finally, before the amused eyes of the spectators, Roy cleared the table and gloomily piled the contents into the box which had held the tickets. Agatha gave the money to a startled Mrs Bloxby, who said, 'That was quick. And everything gone! A lot of that stuff has turned up year in and year out.'

'Before we go, Aggie,' said Roy, leading her

back to the now empty tombola table, 'sign here, or fence and workmen go right back to London.'

He spread a contract out on the table which bound Agatha to Pedmans for six months starting on the first of October.

She hesitated. She could pay Roy for his time and trouble and send the workmen away. But at that moment she heard James's laugh behind her and turned around. He was chatting to Mary and he had already bought two cakes. Mary was wearing a green-and-white-checked shirt with dark green trousers. Her bright hair gleamed in the sunlight.

Agatha turned away and scrawled her signature on the contract, which Roy seized and stuffed in his pocket. 'Give that box of stuff back to Mrs Bloxby,' said Agatha. 'I don't suppose you want any of it apart from the booze.'

'Not a bit of it. It'll come in handy for Christmas presents. I've got a little staff now.'

'You are conscienceless,' said Agatha. 'When you worked for me, what would you have said if I had given you a set of plastic egg-cups for Christmas?'

'Times are hard.' Roy picked up the box of junk and held it close. 'Let's go.'

'There's that young friend of Agatha's again,' said James to Mary, turning to watch them as they walked away.

Mary laughed. 'Quite a goer is our Agatha.'

'What do you mean by that?' James's face was stiff.

'Oh, come on, James. Get real. I think she's having a little fling.'

'Rubbish. Look, I'd better be getting along.'

James marched off but got waylaid by the vicar, who explained he had found a diary in the vicarage which had been kept by one of the villagers during the Napoleonic wars. Agatha temporarily forgotten, James went along to the vicarage in high excitement. Once there, he pored over the diary with a flat feeling of disappointment. The wars may have been raging across Europe, but all this villager had been interested in was the price of everything from wheat to turnips. It was dreary, it was boring, and it was of no use whatsoever, particularly as the prices of everything in England during that period had already been well documented. Still, he thanked the vicar and said he would take it home and study it further.

As he went into his own front garden, he saw a truck with workmen and that Roy Silver driving off from Agatha's. He wondered for the first time that day if Agatha had been stupid enough to plant out her seedlings. He ran upstairs, opened his bedroom window and leaned out.

He blinked. A great high cedarwood fence had been erected around Agatha's garden. What on earth was she doing? That fence was so high it would surely block out any sunlight. Curiosity got the better of him and he went next door and rang her bell.

Agatha answered the door and looked flustered when she saw him.

'That new fence you've got,' said James, 'will block out all sunlight. What are you doing?'

'It's a surprise,' said Agatha. 'You'll see on Open Day. Coffee?'

'Yes, please.' He followed her into the kitchen. The blind was down over the kitchen window, so he could not see the garden.

'Did you plant out your seedlings?' he asked.

'No, do it tomorrow,' said Agatha gruffly.

'That's an enormous fence you've got at the back. Are you sure the sun is going to reach your plants?'

'Oh, yes, don't let's talk about gardening. I'm bored with the subject.'

'Is that why you left the pub without saying goodbye?'

Agatha opened her mouth to say crossly that she did not think her going would be noticed, particularly by him, but a new wisdom made her say instead, 'I just remembered I had forgotten to feed the cats. By the way, I'll be leaving the village for a bit in the autumn.'

'Why?'

76

'Pedmans, that firm I sold out to, have coaxed me back for six months. May as well make some money.'

He looked surprised. 'I thought you had put all that life behind you.' His eyes sparkled. 'I know what it is. There isn't any gory murder to keep you occupied.'

'I'm used to being busy, and there's not much for me here.'

There was something a trifle lost and wistful at the back of Agatha's small eyes which made him say, 'That was rather a disastrous dinner we had. What about another one? There's a new restaurant just off the Evesham road, just outside Evesham. What about trying it?'

The old Agatha would have gushed. The new Agatha said quietly, 'That would be nice. When?'

'What about tonight?'

'Lovely.'

'Good. I'll call for you at seven. I've got to go now. I promised to see Mary about something.'

But the fact that he was leaving to see Mary could not spoil Agatha's sunny mood for the rest of the day. By evening, she was in a high state of excitement. When the phone rang at ten minutes to seven, she looked at it in irritation and then decided not to answer it. Nothing was going to stop her walking out of that door with James at seven. The phone rang for quite a long time and then fell silent. Seven came and went while she sat and fidgeted, handbag on her lap.

Then the doorbell went, and with a little sigh of relief, she went to answer it. James Lacey stood there. His face was pale and his eyes glittered feverishly.

'I'm sorry, Agatha,' he said. 'I'll need to cancel our dinner. I've been so ill. I've been to the doctor and he is treating me for food poisoning.'

'Perhaps if you had something to eat you would feel better?' asked Agatha, willing him to recover.

'No, no. I just want to go to bed. I feel like hell. Another time.' And he went off.

Agatha retreated indoors and sat down feeling lost and empty. She had become friends with Mary but now she almost hated her. Mary had entertained James earlier. She had probably slipped him something. Her common sense tried to tell her she was being silly, but her emotions were in a turmoil and she felt she could not bear to have anything to do with Mary again.

Chapter Four

Despite Agatha's determination not to have anything to do with Mary, a village is a small place and one cannot ignore people the way one can in the city. She could not hold out against Mary's friendliness, and although James had not repeated his dinner invitation, Agatha felt she no longer had any grounds for silly jealousy.

And then a series of crimes happened, which was to initially draw the villagers together and then drive them apart, as suspicion and fear crept into their normally quiet lives.

Mrs Mason found that her prize dahlias had been uprooted and mangled and stamped into the ground. Mrs Bloxby's roses had been poisoned by weedkiller, and most of James Lacey's flowers were no more. Some maniac had doused his garden with petrol and set it alight. And the crimes went on. A nasty hole was dug in Miss Simms's lawn. Even that old couple, the Boggles, had black paint sprayed on their white rosebush, turning all the roses black. Fred Griggs, the local policeman, tried to cope on his own, but as the list of incidents grew, the CID were called in from Mircester, and so Bill Wong was back at work in Carsely again.

At first, when the crimes against gardens had just started, the Red Lion did a roaring trade, as the customers gathered together to discuss the events, all deciding that hooligans from Birmingham had been descending on the village during the night and spitefully wrecking the gardens. Groups of villagers patrolled the streets at night armed with shotguns. There was a wartime feeling of a community working together against a common evil. It was Mrs Boggle, crouched over a pint in the Red Lion one evening, who administered the first blow to this cosy feeling. 'Reckon this would never have happened in the old days. In the old days we didn't have no newcomers.'

Her elderly voice had been loud. There was a sudden silence. Agatha, standing with Mary at the bar and hoping despite all her good resolutions that James Lacey would come in, felt an almost tangible chill creeping into the communal warmth. And then no one wanted to discuss the outrages with them. Not all at once, but gradually, people began to leave and Agatha and Mary were left alone at the bar.

'Oh, dear,' said Mary. 'That wretched old woman.'

The next day, Agatha had more to worry about. Bill Wong called, but not for coffee and a chat. 'I have to inspect everyone's gardens, Agatha,' he said apologetically. 'You know, to see if anyone's been using more weedkiller than they ought or got used cans of petrol stacked anywhere.'

'We're friends,' protested Agatha desperately. 'You know me. I wouldn't do anything like that!'

'But I'm an honest cop, Agatha, and you can't expect me to lie. Besides, what have you got to hide?'

'But –'

'Agatha!'

Miserably, Agatha led him through to the kitchen and unlocked the back door. Bill stared in amazement at the bare garden and then up at the high fence.

'What on earth are you doing?' he asked. 'I thought you were a member of the horticultural society.'

'Look, don't put this in your report, Bill. I planted out my seedlings and they were all killed by the frost. That friend of mine, Roy Silver, put a fence around the garden so that no one could see in. Then just before Open Day –

you know, when the village gardens are open to the public – he was going to come down with a load of plants.'

'Cheating again? Led to disaster last time,' said Bill, referring to the time when Agatha had bought a quiche instead of baking it for a village competition and one of the judges had dropped dead of cowbane poisoning.

'There's no prize for Open Day,' said Agatha. 'I just wanted the garden to look pretty. And you're looking for weedkiller and things. You don't need to put any of this in your report.'

'No, so long as you don't have anything incriminating. But I thought you had grown out of this sort of behaviour.' Bill looked at her severely, and although he was only in his twenties he made Agatha feel like a guilty child.

'Don't moralize. Just get on with your search.'

'I'll look in the greenhouse because I can see there's nothing else in the garden.'

Bill searched the greenhouse and then came back. He snapped his notebook shut. 'That's all, then.'

'Stay for a coffee.'

'No, I don't think so. I'm disappointed in you, Agatha.'

'But I could help you find out who's been doing this.'

'Just keep out of it and leave it to the police.'

Bill marched through the house and let himself out by the front door without saying goodbye.

Sod him, thought Agatha, hurt and angry. I'll show him. I'll find out who's been doing this. Two murder cases he couldn't have solved without my help, and this is all the thanks I get. A tear rolled down one cheek and she scrubbed it away with her sleeve.

The atmosphere in the village grew sourer as suspicion began to centre on Mary Fortune, of all people. Although Agatha and James Lacey were also incomers, for some reason Mary became the target, a fact that puzzled Agatha Raisin, for Mary had initially endeared herself to the villagers. The fact that Mary was a superb gardener and that *her* garden had not been touched added fuel to the suspicions. Doris Simpson, Agatha's excellent cleaner, had been sworn to secrecy about the fenced garden and Bill Wong had not said anything; still, suspicion should have centred on this incomer, who had a garden that nobody saw, yet it was Mary who was the target.

'I don't understand it,' said Mary plaintively one morning when she called on Agatha. 'After all I've done for this village!' And Agatha, despite her simmering jealousy of Mary, could not understand it either. And yet, when she went

83

with Mary to the pub, the hostility towards Mary was evident. 'I'm sick of this,' said Mary. 'As soon as the horticultural show is over, I'm leaving.'

'Surely they won't be having one now,' said Agatha. 'It's not fair on the ones who have had their gardens destroyed.'

'Oh, all of them, even James, claim they have salvaged enough to at least put one bloom in for the show. What about you, Agatha? What are you submitting?'

'I won't bother,' said Agatha, thinking guiltily of her bare garden. She had been going to buy something and put it in as her own, but the memory of Bill Wong's disappointment in her still rankled.

There was a final crime just before the competition which was out of line with the rest. Mr Bernard Spott, the chairman of the horticultural society, that elderly and scholarly gentleman, had his magnificent goldfish poisoned. They were found floating belly-up in the garden pond, as dead as doornails.

As the show approached, the sourness in the village increased but then abated somewhat when it was announced that Mrs Bloxby was to be judge and present the prize for the best. No one could suspect Mrs Bloxby of being anything but fair.

Agatha invited Roy Silver down for the weekend. She did not want to go to the show without any support. James talked to her frequently and even called around for the occasional coffee, but he always seemed preoccupied and somewhat distant and never issued any more invitations to dinner.

Despite her good intentions, Agatha cracked before the show and drove to a nursery in Oxfordshire and bought a magnificent rosebush, almost blue roses, called Blue Moon. She did not even have to take it out of the pot because other contestants had potted their exhibits.

'You're learning, or getting back your old evil ways,' said Roy. 'Love it, love it. You'll be a credit to Pedmans.'

And that made Agatha suddenly wish she had not decided to cheat. But old habits die hard and she forgot about her guilt as she walked along to the competition with Roy. The day was sunny and warm. 'Do you know,' she said, 'I think whoever was playing these nasty tricks was doing it to put other people out of the running. I've a feeling that when this show is over, the village will return to its normal calm.' She had told Roy about the attacks on the gardens.

The band was playing, the hall was full of villagers, and the air was heavy with the scent of flowers. There were also stands of home-made cakes and jam and the tea-room at the side of the hall was doing a brisk business. Roses of all kinds seemed to be the favourite flower. To Agatha's delight, the prize was to be a silver cup. It would look good on her mantelpiece.

Mrs Bloxby began the judging. She walked from exhibit to exhibit, a pair of horn-rimmed glasses on the end of her nose. She stopped before Agatha's and stood very silent for a moment. Then she looked directly at Agatha with her mild questioning eyes. To Agatha's horror, she felt herself beginning to blush all over. The blush started somewhere at her toes and worked its way up to her face in a great surging tide of red.

Roy suddenly muttered under his breath as Mrs Bloxby moved on and he leaned past Agatha and whipped something off the pot. 'What are you doing?' whispered Agatha.

'There was a little label there with the name of the nursery,' hissed Roy.

'Oh, God. Do you think Mrs Bloxby saw anything?'

'Probably not. But you're slipping, dearie. The crafty old Aggie would never have done anything stupid like that.'

'Let's get a cup of tea,' said Agatha. 'It's too agonizing waiting for a decision.'

In the tea-room, James and Mary were sitting side by side. They saw Agatha and Roy and called them over.

'At least nothing awful has happened,' said

Agatha as she sat down and Roy went up to the counter to buy them both tea. 'I almost expected some maniac with a flame-thrower to burst into the hall.'

'That little Chink friend of yours has been poking around all our gardens,' said Mary languidly.

Agatha looked at her in irritation. 'I sometimes can't make you out, Mary,' she said. 'You're as nice as anything and then you come out with some rather nasty remark. My friend, Bill Wong, is half Chinese. His mother is from Evesham. I do not like hearing anyone call him a little Chink.'

Mary laughed. 'I think you're sweet on him, Agatha. I think I've found the Chink in your armour.' Her glance moved to the approaching Roy. 'You do like them young.'

'Don't bitch me, Mary,' said Agatha, her eyes narrowing. 'I've been bitched by experts.'

There was a silence as Roy set down the teacups. His eyes darted from one to the other. 'Well, aren't we the jolly party,' he said. 'Who do you think is going to win?'

'I'm fed up with the whole thing,' said James Lacey, suddenly angry. 'This used to be one of the best villages in Gloucestershire, the friendliest. Now it's all spoilt!' He left abruptly, slamming the door behind him.

'What was all that about?' asked Mary, her blue eyes at their widest.

'You didn't help the general atmosphere by your remarks,' retorted Agatha.

Mary suddenly smiled, a warm smile. 'I'm sorry, Agatha. You're right. I was bitchy. I'm just knocked off beam by all the hostility towards me in this village. It's just so unfair.'

'Why you?' asked Roy.

'I'm an incomer.'

'So's Aggie here.'

'Well, they've singled me out as the mad garden destroyer. After all I've done!'

'They'll get over it,' said Agatha.

'I don't think I'll wait around to see it happen.' Mary got to her feet. 'I'd better go and make my peace with James.'

'She a friend of yours?' asked Roy when Mary had left.

'Yes, I suppose she is. She was a bit bitchy while you were getting the tea, but I suppose the strain is getting to her.'

'She looks like megabitch-woman to me,' said Roy. 'You're slipping, Aggie. In London, you would have given old plastic face a wide berth.'

But in London, thought Agatha, all those years in London, I didn't know how to make friends. My work was my friend. So I try to make the best of people.

'It's different in a village,' she said. 'It's not like London, when you don't even know your neighbours.' A London, she thought, suddenly and bleakly, that she would be returning to all too soon. Would James miss her? Probably wouldn't notice she had gone.

The microphone in the hall gave that preparatory whine that it always seems to make at amateur functions, and then Mrs Bloxby's voice could be heard announcing that she was about to name the prizewinner.

Agatha and Roy hurried into the hall and joined the crowd standing in front of the platform.

Mrs Bloxby picked up the silver cup. I wonder if they will engrave it for me, thought Agatha, or whether I have to get it done myself.

'The first prize,' said Mrs Bloxby, 'goes to . . .'

I should have prepared a little speech, thought Agatha.

'. . . Mr Bernard Spott for his roses. Come up, Mr Spott.'

Probably poisoned his goldfish himself to make him look innocent, Agatha decided in a sudden rush of bile. Probably damaged all those other gardens to put everyone else out of the running.

But as elderly Mr Spott, his face pink with gratification, went up to the platform, her new better nature took over and she began to applaud, and everyone else followed suit.

Mr Spott took a folded piece of paper out of his pocket and went up to the microphone.

'Friends,' he began, and then droned on about how grateful he was.

'The old bugger had a speech prepared,' marvelled Roy.

Mr Spott went on for fifteen minutes, until Mrs Bloxby coughed and pointed to her watch.

'And the second prize,' said Mrs Bloxby, 'is to Mr James Lacey for his delphiniums.'

'I thought someone executed the scorched-earth policy on his garden,' said Roy. 'Maybe he bought something, only *he* remembered to take the name of the nursery off the pot.'

'Shhh!' admonished Agatha. Surely she would get third prize.

'And the third prize goes to Miss Simms for her Busy Lizzies.'

'Rats,' said Agatha. At least neither James nor Miss Simms felt obliged to make speeches.

'That's that,' said Roy. 'Fun over. Let's go somewhere for a late lunch.'

'Perhaps James might come to lunch with us?' suggested Agatha.

'Get real, Aggie,' said Roy brutally. 'He's not interested in you.'

Agatha felt old and depressed as she followed Roy out of the hall. Her life stretched before her one long and dusty road to the grave. Nothing would ever happen again to make her happy or excited or interested. She looked back at the villagers and felt like an outsider, a stranger, belonging nowhere except perhaps to the Birmingham slum from which she had sprung. And then Miss Simms, flushed and excited, caught up with her. 'You've got a special ticket on your roses, Mrs Raisin.'

Surprised, Agatha turned back. There was a little red card in front of her rosebush. Excited, she bent down and read the commendation. 'Mrs Agatha Raisin, special commendation for ingenuity.'

Roy read it at the same time. 'Oh, wicked Mrs Bloxby, Aggie. Come away. A plate of steak-and-kidney pie will make you feel lots better.'

'You know, Roy,' said Agatha as she drove him into Oxford to catch the train on Sunday evening, 'I think you should forget this scam about bringing all those plants down. Just do me a favour and send the workmen back to take the top part of the fence off. I'll buy some plants from a nursery myself and let everyone see me planting them and I won't open my garden to the public.'

'Oh, come on. Just because you were stupid enough to leave that nursery label on the pot doesn't mean you're going to fail. I'll be down myself with the truck at two in the morning. Bingo, instant garden. You know yourself nothing moves in Carsely during the night. Besides, I've got more news for you. Pedmans is paying for the lot.'

'Why?'

'It's instead of a golden hello.'

'You mean that little ferret, Wilson, knows I am going to cheat?'

'Of course not. As far as he is concerned, you just want to beautify your garden. He's mad keen to get you, Aggie. And the stuff is going to be magnificent.'

Agatha felt herself weaken. Nothing could go wrong. And Mrs Bloxby might be forced to think she had made a mistake. She did not want to lose respect in the eyes of Mrs Bloxby.

'Oh, all right,' she said. 'But you'd better be there on the great day to help me out.'

The next night found her among a large crowd in the Red Lion. It was the publican's, John Fletcher's, birthday, and he was dispensing free drinks all round. With a lift of the heart, Agatha saw James and went to join him. 'I didn't know it was John's birthday,' she said guiltily, eyeing the pile of presents on the bar. 'Why didn't anyone tell me?'

'They probably thought you knew. You were here last year, after all.'

'Perhaps I should go home and see if I have anything in the house I can give him,' said Agatha, yet not wanting to leave James's side. She could hardly believe that Mary was not there to monopolize his attention, which she did so well.

'Congratulations on your prize,' she said. 'I didn't think there was anything left in your back garden after the attack on it.'

'Well, you can hardly see into it now,' he said. 'Not with that great fence you've got around it. Why such a high fence?'

'I'm keeping my plants sheltered.'

He looked puzzled. 'I don't know how you even managed to grow those roses. That must be what Mrs Bloxby meant by ingenuity.'

Agatha did not normally like her conversations with James to be interrupted, but she looked up in relief as Mr Galloway, a large Scotsman who ran a garage in a neighbouring village, leaned over and said, 'I was talking to Fred Griggs and he says they still don't have a clue who was responsible for wrecking those gardens. I thought you would have tracked down the culprit by now, Mrs Raisin.'

'I'll maybe get to work on it.' Agatha preened a little. 'The police don't seem to be doing much of a job.'

'Where's Mary?' asked James.

Mr Galloway scratched his thatch of hair.

'I dunno,' he said. 'Maybe herself is prettifying to make an appearance.'

'It is odd, all the same,' pursued James to Agatha's distress. 'I'm unhappy about this stupid dislike for Mary. To think she had anything to do with wrecking gardens is madness.'

'Not as if *she* won any prizes,' commented Agatha maliciously.

'That was a strange thing,' said Mr Galloway. 'We all thought herself would take the first with those dahlias of hers.'

'I thought no one wanted her to win,' said James.

'Aye, but Mrs Bloxby was doing the judging and Mrs Bloxby woundnae be fashed by gossip.'

'Another drink, James? Mr Galloway?' Agatha felt they had talked about Mary for long enough.

But just as Mr Galloway was beginning to say, 'That's very kind of you,' James rose to his feet. 'I think I'll walk up to Mary's cottage and see if she's coming.'

Agatha rose as well. 'I'll go with you. Get you a drink when I return, Mr Galloway.'

As they walked together through the still-balmy summer night, Agatha could not help wishing they were walking out together and not going to visit some blonde. The gossip in the village relayed by Doris Simpson was that Mary and James were only casual friends and that he did not visit her cottage or take her out for dinner any more. Agatha began to wonder what she really knew of Mary. Jealousy had coloured her opinion, clouded her judgement. So, she had decided, let's look at Mary objectively. Take jealous thoughts away, and Agatha had to admit to herself that Mary was a very attractive woman with a certain warmth and charm. And yet sometimes, through that warmth and charm, there sparked little darts of . . . malice? Uncomfortable remarks. The remark she had made about Bill had been downright bitchy, and it was not like her to slip up like that.

James looked down at her quizzically. 'Not like you to be so quiet.'

'I was thinking about Mary,' said Agatha. 'I was thinking that I don't really know her very well.'

'That's surprising. I thought the pair of you were the best of friends.'

'Well . . .' Agatha realized with surprise that she had accepted Mary's friendship only to look for ways to make sure that the coolness between her and James stayed that way. 'What do you really know of her?' she asked.

'Come to think of it, not much. I know she was married because she's got a daughter studying at Oxford, St Crispin's, I think.'

'I've never seen her daughter, and she never talks about her.'

'The daughter never visits her, even in the holidays. I assumed there was some sort of family rift there, so I didn't ask any questions. I also assumed that what you saw was what you got – perfect cook, perfect gardener, perfectly turned out. Then she has charm, and charm always stops you from seeing the person underneath.'

Not like me, thought Agatha. What you see is definitely what you get. And she longed for charm or mysterious depths.

'They were approaching Mary's cottage. 'No lights,' said James. 'Maybe she's gone out, Oxford or somewhere.'

'That's another thing,' said Agatha. 'She never does leave the village, except perhaps when she is dining with you.'

'Well, let's see if she's at home.'

Instead of going around the back, as was usual village practice except at homes like Agatha's, they walked up through the front garden where flowers, bleached by the moonlight, crowded the borders on either side of the lawn. The air was heavy with the scent of the flowers. They walked into the front porch. James rang the bell, which echoed off into the dark silence of the house.

Down in the road behind them, a young couple walked home. The girl laughed, a high, shrill giggle. Their footsteps and voices died away, leaving night silence behind.

'That's that,' said Agatha cheerfully. 'We've

done our bit for community life. Now back to the pub.' With any luck, she thought, the crowd might have thinned out and she could have James to herself.

He hesitated. He tried the door handle. It turned easily and the door swung open. 'She might be ill.' He walked inside and Agatha reluctantly followed him. He fumbled around for the light switch in the hall. With a little click the small hall became flooded with light, intensifying the odd feeling of emptiness, of loneliness, in the house. They walked through the rooms, switching on the lights. No one in either the living-room, dining-room or kitchen.

James ran up the stairs, calling, 'Mary! Mary!' Agatha stood in the hall, waiting uneasily. She had never considered herself a fey or even a sensitive person, but as she stood there she began to feel a creeping unease.

'Not home,' said James, coming back down the narrow staircase.

'There's her conservatory at the back,' said Agatha. 'We may as well make a proper job of it.' Afterwards she was to wonder at her sudden persistence when a moment before all she had wanted to do was forget about the whole thing and return to the pub with James. After a brief and sharp struggle with the planning authorities, Mary had gained permission to have a small conservatory attached to the back of the house.

They walked through the kitchen and James opened the conservatory door and switched on the light. A wave of steamy moist air greeted them. Mary grew tropical plants. They walked into the middle of the conservatory and stood still, shoulder to shoulder. All was still. 'Let's go,' said James.

And then Agatha said in a choked voice, 'Look! Look over there!'

And James looked.

Someone had planted Mary Fortune.

Her head was not visible; it was covered in earth. Someone had hung her upside down by her ankles and buried her head in earth in a large earthenware pot. There were hooks on the ceiling beams for hanging plant pots. Someone had tied her ankles with rope and slung her up on to one of these hooks. She was dressed in that inevitable colour of green; green sandals, green blouse, and green shorts.

'Cut her down!' Agatha's voice was harsh with horror.

But James was bending over Mary and feeling for any life in the pulse at her neck and in her wrist.

He straightened up. 'Leave everything as it is for the police. She's been murdered and she's stone-dead.'

'Murder!'

'Pull yourself together, Agatha,' he said sharply. 'She didn't plant herself. I'll phone.'

He left the conservatory. Agatha gave one last horrified look at the body and scrambled out after him on shaky legs.

James was in the living-room. He called Fred Griggs and then sat down heavily on the sofa and clutched his thick hair with both hands. 'It's terrible . . . terrible,' he said. 'I slept with her, you know.'

Agatha, already overset, sat down and began to cry weakly. 'Don't cry,' he said gruffly. 'She cannot feel anything now.'

But Agatha was crying from a mixture of shock and shame. All her feelings for James now seemed like some sort of dismal schoolgirl crush. She had always thought that he led a monkish life, shy of women, always unattached, and because she herself had not indulged in an affair for some time, she had found it easier to dream about him as romantically as a schoolgirl. She had been jealous of his friendship with Mary, but she had considered it just that – friendship, with a bit of light flirtation, nothing more. But he had lain in Mary's bed and in Mary's arms. Her mind writhed under the weight of her miserable thoughts.

PC Griggs lumbered in. He looked like a village policeman, stolid, red-faced. One almost expected him to say, ''Ello, 'ello, 'ello. What 'ave

99

we 'ere?' But he was a shrewd and clever man in his slow way.

'Where's the body?' he asked.

James unfolded his length from the sofa. 'I'll show you.'

Agatha looked longingly at the drinks trolley in the corner. She felt a stiff brandy might help her to pull herself together. Just as she was wondering whether she could risk pouring one by wrapping a handkerchief around the bottle, the CID arrived. Detective Sergeant Bill Wong was part of the group. Behind them came more cars. Pathologist, doctor, forensic team, police cameraman, and the press from the local newspaper, whose enterprising editor listened in on the police radio.

Bill Wong looked at Agatha's tear-stained face and, thinking she was mourning Mary, said with quick compassion, 'You go on home, Agatha. We'll be along to take a statement later. You found the body?'

'Yes, me and James Lacey.'

'Is he here?'

'Yes, with the body.'

'Right. He'll do for now. I'll get one of my men to take you home.'

And Agatha was at such a low point that she let a policeman put a strong arm about her and lead her away.

Chapter Five

Agatha sat nursing a glass of brandy in one hand and a lighted cigarette in the other. She noticed with a numb clinical interest that her hands were shaking slightly. She wished now she had stayed at Mary's. Her home was so quiet under its heavy thatched roof, unusually quiet. Mostly the old house creaked comfortably as it settled down for the night.

Who could have done such a thing? What had she ever known of Mary? What had she ever really known of James Lacey, for that matter? He was intelligent, handsome, in his mid-fifties, a retired colonel who had settled in the country to write military history. They had investigated a previous murder together. She knew he could be resourceful and quite ruthless in dangerous circumstances. They had talked together quite a lot then, but about books and plays, about the murder case, about people in the village. What really made him tick? Would *he* be capable of murder?

But whoever had done the murder had probably also mined those gardens and she could not believe for a minute that James would do something as petty and spiteful as that. It all centred on gardening, of that she was sure. Therefore, her mind ran on, whoever had destroyed the gardens and poisoned Mr Spott's fish and then murdered Mary was quite mad, and viciously so. It had not been enough just to knife Mary or strangle her. Someone had been evil enough to want her humiliated in death. Please, God, let it be someone from Mary's past.

The sound of a car drawing up outside interrupted her thoughts. She stubbed out her cigarette and carefully put her brandy glass down on a side-table, noticing with an odd sort of pride that her hands had stopped shaking. She went to answer the door. Bill Wong stood there with a policewoman.

'I'll take an initial statement from you, Agatha,' he said, 'and then I would like you to report to headquarters in Mircester tomorrow while we go through it again. I have asked Mr Lacey to come as well, so perhaps you can travel in together.'

Agatha led Bill and the policewoman into the living-room. 'Would you like coffee?'

The policewoman sat down demurely on a hard chair in the corner of the room and flicked open her notebook. 'Not this time,' said Bill.

'No tape recorder?'

'We'll tape your statement tomorrow, have it typed up and read it back to you. So begin at the beginning.'

Agatha spoke of the start of the evening in the pub and how James had become anxious over Mary's non-appearance. She described how they had called at the cottage and found the door unlocked, gone inside, searched, and then found the body in the small conservatory.

'It would take someone of considerable strength to hoist a dead body up like that,' ventured Agatha.

'Perhaps,' said Bill. 'The forensic chaps have taken the rope away, along with every speck of dust in that house. It's amazing what they can find out these days. Now who else was in the pub when you left with Mr Lacey?'

Agatha wrinkled her brow. 'Let me see. James and I were talking to Mr Galloway. Miss Simms was over at the bar with old Mr Spott. Mrs Mason and her husband were at the bar as well, and those pests, the Boggles, were complaining about the strength of the beer in another corner. In front of the fire was my cleaner, Doris Simpson, and her husband.' She half closed her eyes and continued to list the villagers. 'Oh, and there was one stranger, on his own, at the far left of the bar.'

'What did he look like?'

'Early twenties, jeans, designer stubble, thick sandy hair worn in a pony-tail, nondescript face. You know, two eyes, one nose, one mouth. I only noticed him because he was the only stranger there. He seemed to be waiting for someone. This is all a vague impression. You see, I was talking to James.'

'Yes, I see what you mean,' said Bill with a faint twinkle in his eyes. 'Now, when you both approached Mrs Fortune's cottage, did you meet anyone?'

'I don't think so. Everyone in this village says hello. I was thinking about Mary, as a matter of fact.'

'Mrs Fortune? What were you thinking?'

'I was thinking that although we were friends, I knew so little about her. I mean, she was all charm and warmth and then she would come out with some sort of bitchy remark.'

'Such as?'

'She called you a Chink.'

'Nothing to what I get back at the station. It's probably the sort of thing she usually said.'

'No, she was out to be nasty. I was surprised that she was so overtly bitchy. I mean, often there was something you just couldn't put your finger on.'

'Lacey must have known her better than anyone.'

'Why?' demanded Agatha defensively.

'Well known in the village he was romancing her.'

'Nothing to it.' Agatha's heart had begun to hammer against her ribs. 'He took her out for a few dinners and then that stopped. They were just friends.'

Bill looked at her distressed face. Lacey had been quite open about the fact that he and Mrs Fortune had been lovers earlier in the year, but all at once he could not bring himself to tell Agatha that.

The doorbell went. 'I'll get it,' he said.

He answered the door and then came back followed by Mrs Bloxby, who was carrying a small travel bag.

'I thought you would feel better if someone stayed here with you for the night, Mrs Raisin.'

Agatha's eyes filled with tears again and she blinked them away.

'That's all for now,' said Bill. 'Come along to the police station at ten tomorrow. Get a good night's sleep. I'll call on Lacey and tell him to pick you up.'

Agatha escorted Bill and the policewoman to the door. Bill smiled at her. 'Not like London, hey?'

'They have lots of murders in London.'

'I didn't mean that. I meant that there would

be no Mrs Bloxby in London to think of sitting with you.'

'Oh, that. See you tomorrow.'

Agatha returned to Mrs Bloxby. 'Come through to the kitchen and I'll make some tea.'

'Yes, but I'll make it. And then you'd better go to bed. What a dreadful experience. News travels fast here, but I found it hard to believe. Mrs Griggs, Fred's wife, phoned me to tell me that someone had *planted* Mrs Fortune.'

'Yes, it was horrible,' said Agatha. 'She had been strung up by the ankles and her head had been buried in a big flowerpot. And she was wearing that damn green like she always did. We didn't see her at first because of that green, because . . .' Agatha began to shake.

'There now. There now. I'll just put the kettle on. I am very distressed as well, although I did not have such a vile experience as you, Mrs Raisin.'

Agatha smiled weakly. 'We should not be so formal with each other. I think you should call me Agatha and I will call you . . .?'

'Margaret.'

'Were you fond of Mary?'

'It's not that.' Mrs Bloxby's thin hands busied themselves putting tea in the teapot and filling it with boiling water. 'I let my personal feelings interfere with my judging of the horticultural show and I have never done that before.'

Agatha blinked. 'I find that hard to believe. Why?'

The vicar's wife filled two mugs with hot tea, took milk out of the fridge and waited until they were both seated at the kitchen table. She stirred sugar into her tea and then said slowly, 'I was one of Mrs Fortune's admirers at first. It is so pleasant when a newcomer involves herself in helping out with church and village activities. She called at the vicarage quite a lot. She used to flirt with Alf.'

Not for the first time, Agatha considered Alf quite an unsuitable name for a vicar. 'I did not mind because Mary Fortune is . . . was . . . a well-travelled, pretty woman, of the kind, I thought, who flirts automatically. Then she wanted Alf to take her confession. Well, our church is quite *low* and Alf does not have a confessional, but he will always listen to any parishioner in trouble, so he agreed to an interview with her in his study. I do not know what happened, but he told me afterwards that he considered her not a very nice woman and somewhat unstable. Then, when she called, he always found some excuse to leave the house.

'Mrs Fortune began to make little remarks to me, little disparaging remarks. You know, it was a pity I had let myself go. She could recommend a good hairdresser and so on. I have varicose veins, but I wear my skirts long so people don't

107

usually notice, but Mrs Fortune did. And then the next time I saw her, she would be all sweetness and light and friendship, but the poison began to seep in and I began to feel diminished and dowdy. To my horror, I began to dislike her and I never usually dislike people very strongly. One cannot like everybody and I sometimes find the Boggles, say, a sore trial, but there was something about her that got under my skin.

'She would smile at me slowly and pityingly. She would ask how many countries I had visited, and Alf and I have not been abroad in *years*.'

Agatha began to feel better. It was a relief in a way to find that Mrs Bloxby, whom Agatha had hitherto regarded as a saint, was capable of normal human feelings.

An idea came to her and she leaned forward eagerly. 'It must be like being blackmailed or conned. That's it. Conned.'

'What do you mean?'

'I remember reading a case in the papers where a chap in a village had tricked various people out of their savings by pretending to be a stockbroker. He wasn't very good at it and the first couple he had conned quickly found out about it. But they did not take him to court. They were too ashamed of being gulled, don't you see. So he was able to go on for a bit, tricking other people.

'Now, when people talked to you about Mary,

I am sure you murmured something nice because to say you did not like her would mean you would have to explain why, and the very explanation would make you feel more diminished. I bet she riled more than you. Why did you tell me, of all people?'

Mrs Bloxby looked at her in mild surprise. 'You never judge or condemn, Agatha. I suppose that's it.'

Only in my head, and nearly all the time, thought Agatha ruefully.

And then somehow it was easy for her to say, 'James was having an affair with Mary.'

'So I gathered.'

'But no one said anything to me! James told me last night.'

'It's well known you are a friend of his,' said Mrs Bloxby tactfully. 'People would assume that you knew.' She knew that the reason had been that people did not want to hurt Agatha. 'But there's a thing. Although he stayed on friendly terms with her, he definitely cooled off her when you arrived back. It might be worth finding out why. I feel if we all knew Mary Fortune better, then we could learn who murdered her and why. You will be finding out, will you not? It is not only the murder, you see, that destroys and rips apart the tranquillity of the village, but the intrusions of the press. Such a colourful murder, you see. The press are already arriving in droves.

Sooner or later, someone is going to check the press library and find out about your previous investigations and your phone will start ringing and your doorbell.'

As if in reply, the doorbell shrilled. 'I will deal with it,' said Mrs Bloxby. Agatha heard the vicar's wife open the door, then the murmur of voices, then Mrs Bloxby saying firmly, 'Mrs Raisin has had a bad shock. She is not to be disturbed,' and then the slam of the door.

'Thank you,' said Agatha when Mrs Bloxby returned to the kitchen, although her vanity stabbed her. If she had been on her own, she would probably have invited the press in.

Then the phone rang. Without asking permission, Mrs Bloxby answered it, repeated that Mrs Raisin was not well enough to be interviewed, and then returned. 'I pulled the phone out from the wall. You will not be disturbed again. I'll just go upstairs and unplug the extension as well.'

Agatha rose to her feet and opened her mouth to say she was well able to deal with the press, but her knees trembled and she felt weak and shaky. 'You know,' she said, 'I think I *will* go to sleep.'

But half an hour later when she closed her eyes, visions of James in the arms of Mary Fortune swam in her mind, and with a great effort she willed herself to go to sleep to make all those nasty pictures go away.

James called for her at nine the following morning. In an obscure way, Agatha was glad the old elation at the thought of going out with him had gone. She felt like a silly middle-aged woman. She had once had a crush, when she was at school, on one of the older boys, and she had behaved with James Lacey just like that. Her distress at learning of his affair with Mary had gone, to be replaced with a strange kind of relief to be free of what had gradually been becoming an obsession. She had put on the minimum of make-up and a plain white blouse, a tailored skirt, and low-heeled shoes. 'We'll take my car,' said James. 'Silly for both of us to drive separately.'

They drove off. The silence lasted all the way up to the A44. Then James said, 'Have you been thinking about it?'

'The murder? Of course. Thought of nothing else.'

'Maybe after we have made our statements, we should have lunch and talk about it.' He glanced sideways, wondering at the unusually silent response. 'If you want to,' he added finally.

'Yes, all right,' said Agatha. Her reluctance came from a new desire to stay free of any emotional entanglement, that is, her emotional entanglement with James. She could never believe now that at any time he had felt anything warmer for her than friendship.

'Good, then we'll leave the talking until then.'

At the police headquarters in Mircester, James and Agatha were interviewed together and then separately. This time Agatha was not interviewed by Bill Wong. She asked for him and learned he was in Carsely with the other detectives who were investigating the case.

She had her statement read over to her and signed it. She had been asked if there had been any man in Mary's life and had replied with a firm negative. It was up to James to tell them if he wanted to.

She waited in the entrance hall of the police station for James and was almost beginning to wonder if they had arrested him on suspicion when his tall figure appeared.

'Well, now, what sort of food do you want to eat?' James asked.

'Something light,' said Agatha. 'I'm still on a diet of sorts.'

He glanced down at her. 'Yes, it shows. There's a new place in the square. They do very good salads and things like that and the tables are set well apart, so we don't have to worry about anyone overhearing us.'

They walked together across the square. The sunny day was now overcast and an irritating, busy little wind tugged at Agatha's hair and blew swirls of dust about their feet. It had been an unusually dry summer and to date the gardeners had complained about the need for the constant watering of plants.

The restaurant was quiet and they were given a table at the window. Agatha asked for a Caesar salad as a main course and James ordered grilled steak and fried potatoes and onion rings.

'Now,' he began, 'have you thought of anything?'

Agatha hesitated. Before she would cheerfully have repeated everything Mrs Bloxby had told her, laying the confidences of the vicar's wife on the altar of desire, but a queer loyalty stopped her this time, and she said instead, 'I do not think Mary was as popular as I believed her to be.'

'What do you mean?'

'She would never usually say anything directly nasty, but she had a way of making people feel silly and provincial.'

'Perhaps. But not enough to cause murder. It surely has something to do with gardens. In some way it all must tie in with the destruction of the gardens.'

Agatha thought again about Mrs Bloxby and wished she could tell him. Instead, she said,

'Whoever did the murder must have been mentally unbalanced. It was a murder that was planned and thought out, thought out in a sort of smouldering, burning hate. Let's see. You said she had a daughter. She seemed to be a very wealthy woman. Money might be the motive, with the ruin of the gardens and the elaborate way of dealing with the body as a sort of smoke-screen, to make it look as if it had been done by some sort of barmy local. The daughter, you said, is at Oxford University. She could be somewhere abroad during the holidays. But if not, she'll be there today. I wonder if she inherits, and how much. I suppose the press will hang around.'

'Even with a murder like this, only a few days and then they'll leave it to the local men. We could call at Mary's this evening to offer our condolences, if the daughter is there.'

'There'll be press at the gate and a copper on the door,' Agatha pointed out. 'I think we should leave it. I would like to ask some of the people who knew Mary what they really thought of her.'

'She's too recently dead. I don't think anyone's going to come right out at the moment and say they didn't like her.'

Agatha thought of Mrs Bloxby, Mrs Bloxby of all people, whom Mary had managed to rile up. 'I don't know about that,' she said cautiously. She looked at him awkwardly. 'In your situation,

114

you must have known her better than anybody.'

'I didn't, actually. It was a brief fling.'

'And why did the brief fling, as you call it,
come to an end?'

There was silence as their meals were
delivered to the table. When the waitress had
left, James said, 'She came on to me very strongly
and she gave the impression that she was used
to affairs and only wanted to have a good time.
She was charming and she could be very funny.'
He shifted uncomfortably. Mary's humour, he
remembered, had often consisted of being funny
about the villagers. And then Agatha Raisin had
come back among them, squat, blunt Agatha,
who somehow seemed very much a part of the
village. But it was not only that contrast that had
brought about the end of the affair.

'I think,' he said slowly, 'that Mary had begun
to expect marriage. She became very proprietor-
ial.' Then he thought, the sex was competent and
efficient but lacking tenderness or warmth, and
a feeling of revulsion had set in, a feeling of
shame.

'You're not eating your steak,' said Agatha,
looking at it longingly.

'You're not giving me much of a chance.'

She waited until he had eaten several mouth-
fuls and then asked, 'You must have said something to her to break it off.'

'Well, yes, of course. At first I did the usual cowardly masculine thing of staying clear. But then she called at my home and asked me bluntly what I was playing at. I told her it was over. For one awful moment I thought she was going to strike me. Her eyes blazed with pure hate. But the next moment, she laughed and said, "Well, you are quite right. You are not exactly God's gift to women in bed," and . . . and . . . a few other things I do not care to repeat, but all in an amused voice and I did not get angry because I thought I deserved it. We agreed to remain friends. I then began to see more of her again when she became so unpopular in the village. I thought it unkind. She never at any time referred to our affair.'

'Do the police suspect you?'

'A crime of passion? Possibly. They've certainly searched my house thoroughly in the middle of the night looking for bits of rope and examining my clothes and fingernails for traces of earth.'

'So you told them about your affair?'

'Of course.'

So Bill Wong would know, thought Agatha miserably.

'That friend of yours, Bill Wong, took me aside and told me to make sure you did not interfere in the investigation,' said James.

'Considering the success I've had in the past –

we've had in the past,' added Agatha charitably, 'I think that's a bit cheeky.'

'It's because he's fond of you and doesn't want you coming across some maniac of a murderer on your own.'

Agatha thought guiltily of her garden. She sent up a prayer that the CID would not decide to turn over her house. They would see the garden and the sight of that bare garden with the huge high fence might lead them to believe *she* was mentally unstable.

'So,' she said, 'it looks as if we'll have to let the dust settle before we start asking questions.'

They discussed the wreck of the gardens, wondering over and over who in the village could possibly have done such a thing.

When lunch was over, James drove her back to the village. For the first time, he was reluctant to be on his own. It was as if the full horror of Mary's death had hit him for the first time. Agatha was a comfortable, sensible woman. She had not gone in for any of her odd behaviour for ages.

'Why don't you come into my place,' he said. 'I'll light up the computer and we could start putting down some ideas.'

How much I would have enjoyed this only a few days ago, thought Agatha, after she had agreed and followed him into his book-lined living-room, before the fact of his affair with Mary destroyed silly hopeful innocence.

He got them mugs of coffee and switched on the computer.

'Right,' he said. 'Let's start with the attacks on the gardens and list all those whose gardens were destroyed. You didn't suffer.'

'No, but I've got the gates to the back, the one at the side of the house, padlocked.'

'Okay.' He tapped the keys. 'We have the Boggles, Miss Simms, Mrs Mason . . . What is it?' For Agatha had put a hand on his arm.

'What if Mary did it? What if some maddened gardener took his revenge?'

They both looked at each other, both thinking of smooth, cool and plastic Mary creeping around the gardens of Carsely.

'No, I suppose not,' said Agatha.

'I'm afraid we're going to have to adopt your idea and start asking questions. But there's not much we can do until the press thin out.'

'We could go to the pub this evening,' said Agatha hopefully. 'Perhaps when the locals have had a drink or two, they'll open up. I mean, the conversation will be about nothing else.'

'Good idea.' He switched off the computer and smiled at Agatha. 'We'll leave it for the moment.'

To his surprise, Agatha said, 'Right you are. See you later.' She picked up her handbag and left. Before, she would have stayed for as long as possible, ignoring any hints that it was time to go.

Agatha returned to her own home, feeling she had scored a victory over her own juvenile emotions. But her elation was short-lived. For on the doorstep was Bill Wong with a group of men.

'I'm sorry about this, Mrs Raisin,' said Bill formally. 'But we are searching the houses in the village for anyone who knew Mary Fortune, and I'm afraid you can't be excluded.'

'Do you have a search warrant?' asked Agatha feebly.

'Come on, now. You know we can get one. What have you got to hide?'

'Joke,' said Agatha miserably.

It was not the search of the house that troubled her but the dread moment when they moved out into the garden. The small group of men surveyed the neat lawn bordered by well-weeded empty flowerbeds. One scratched his head and said, 'You're a woman after my heart, Mrs Raisin. Can't stand gardening myself. But why such a high fence? I see it's got a top section which could be lifted off and let some of the sun in.'

'I don't like nosy neighbours,' said Agatha defiantly.

'But the only person who could see into your garden is that Mr Lacey next door,' said another. 'Doesn't look the nosy type to me.'

'Just get on with what you have to do,' snapped Agatha and turned on her heel and walked back into the kitchen.

The case simply had to be solved before Open Day or these coppers would still be around and would know she had created an instant garden, that she had cheated.

At last the search was over. Bill Wong stayed behind.

'Has the daughter arrived?' asked Agatha, setting a mug of coffee down in front of him.

'Yes, her name is Beth Fortune and she is studying history at Oxford. She has brought a boyfriend with her who turns out to be the stranger you saw in the pub the day she was killed.'

Agatha's eyes gleamed. 'There's the motive. Beth inherits the lot and gets him to do the dirty work. Does he explain what he was doing in the village?'

'His name is John Derry. He said he had been visiting friends in Warwick, and on the road home he decided to call in at Carsely. He had heard about it from Beth, he said, and was curious to see the village. He had not called on Mary because he had met her once with Beth for a lunch in Oxford and she had taken a dislike to him. We checked with his friends in Warwick and they swear he was there until seven in the evening.'

'And when was Mary killed?'

'They're still finding out when and how.'

'Will you let me know?'

'Agatha, whoever killed Mary Fortune is mad and dangerous. Leave it alone.'

'Okay,' said Agatha meekly, and Bill looked at her suspiciously.

Chapter Six

It had been a week since the murder, and the national press had exhausted every angle. Just when it looked as if interest was dying, some reporter found out that Mrs Josephs, the librarian, had been murdered in that very cottage, and that brought down the feature writers from the noisier tabloids to describe the 'house of death', and the more respectable heavies kept it going by sneering at the Grub Street tabloids and repeating paragraphs out of the 'house of death' stories to prove their point, which was their traditional way of seeming to avoid sensationalism while indulging in it.

But a week is a long time in journalism, and so it was left to the local papers and news agencies to keep tabs on developments while the television people packed up their cameras and sound equipment and satellite dishes and went back to town.

Agatha and James had had a non-productive

evening in the Red Lion and so had decided to let the dust settle before they started on their inquiries. It was James who reported at last to Agatha that the daughter, Beth, and her boyfriend were in residence at Mary's cottage, that the press had gone from the gate and the policeman from the door. It was time to make a move.

There was to be no funeral in the village. The body, when finally released by the pathologist, was to be cremated in Oxford and the ashes scattered out to sea at some point within the regulations of the Ministry of Agriculture and Fisheries. That much, said James, as he sat in Agatha's kitchen, he had gleaned from Mrs Bloxby. He had asked if there was to be a memorial service in the church, and Mrs Bloxby, he said, had been strangely cold and had said that was a matter for Mrs Fortune's family and the villagers to decide.

'It seems,' said Agatha, 'that the villagers will not really say what they thought of Mary until they've been given some time. I think the same applies to you. Mary was nasty to me on several occasions, so it follows she must have been nasty to other people. From what you said, or more from what you did not say, I think she was particularly poisonous to you when you ended the affair, and yet you continued to see her on a friendly basis. Why?'

He hesitated for a long moment, looking down into his coffee cup as if seeking inspiration. Then he looked up with a wry smile and said, 'Shame and guilt. Guilt because I felt I had really hurt her. Shame because I felt I should never have had an affair with such as Mary. Also arrogance. I wanted to persuade myself that she was really all right and that we could be friends. As if any kind of emotional involvement can ever turn into friendship.'

Too right, thought Agatha gloomily, wondering if she would ever get over a feeling of wistfulness when she looked at him.

'There was something else,' he said quietly, 'something I have only realized now. I think that somewhere inside Mary was a capacity for violence.'

'Interesting, but it doesn't get us anywhere,' Agatha pointed out. 'Someone laid violent hands on *her.*'

'But don't you see,' he said eagerly, 'violence can beget violence. And it's usually in the family. We must try to find out where her ex-husband is and whether he is in this country. I gathered she was married in America, in Los Angeles.'

'She said she lived in New York!'

'Well, she may have moved there after the divorce.'

Agatha rose to her feet. 'I think we should get on with making a call on the daughter. Does the daughter know you were making love to her mother?'

James coloured slightly. 'I don't know. I shouldn't think so. I got the impression that mother and daughter were barely on speaking terms.'

'Let's go anyway. Should we take something? Does one usually take something?'

'Flowers or cake? No, I don't think so. Condolences in hushed whispers seem to be the order of the day.'

Agatha left the living-room after shutting the door carefully behind her and let her cats out into the back garden. She winced as she looked at it. The cats made their way to the one patch of sun that had been able to shine over the high fence.

They made their way to Mary's cottage, each thinking of the last time they had walked there together. They went up the front garden to the glassed-in porch that Mary had had built at the front of the house, in addition to the conservatory at the back. In fact, she had altered and changed the cottage so much, it was hard to remember what a poky little place it had seemed when Mrs Josephs lived there.

For a moment after James had rung the bell, Agatha almost expected Mary herself to answer the door. It suddenly seemed incredible that she was dead, that she had been killed in such a macabre way.

But the door was answered by a girl in her early twenties who did not look at all like Mary. She had brown eyes, a sallow skin, a long thin nose, and a quantity of glossy black hair. She was wearing a man's tartan shirt loose over a pair of brief shorts. Her legs were very long, very white, and quite hairy.

'Miss Fortune?' asked James.

'Yes?' The girl looked at him curiously and then her eyes moved to Agatha.

'This is Mrs Agatha Raisin, a friend of your late mother. I am James Lacey, also a friend. We came to offer our condolences.'

She stood back. 'You'd better come in.'

In the living-room, her boyfriend, John Derry, was slouched in an armchair. In the way of modern youth, Beth did not bother introducing them. 'Coffee or tea?' she asked.

'Neither,' said Agatha quickly, not wanting a moment to be lost while Beth disappeared into the kitchen. 'Have the police found out how your mother died?' she asked.

'Someone poisoned her first with weedkiller and then strung her up,' said Beth. Her eyes were dry and her voice hard and rather impatient, with an underlying faint twang of an American accent.

'Don't worry,' said James. 'The police will soon find out who did it.'

'How?' asked John Derry, speaking for the first time.

'There must be loads of clues,' said James. 'There's the rope which tied her, the weedkiller, surely lots of things.'

'The rope,' said Beth, 'was old-fashioned Woolworth's-type clothes-line, probably bought a long time ago, for all you can get now is the plastic stuff. There were no fingerprints at all apart from those of the two who found the body.' Her eyes widened a fraction. 'Oh, that was you two, wasn't it?'

Agatha nodded. There was something almost intimidating about Beth's self-possession. 'Will your father be arriving for the funeral?' she asked.

'Shouldn't think so. He hated Mother.'

'So he's still in America?'

'Yes, Los Angeles.'

'Have you heard from him?'

'He phoned a few days ago and asked if he could help . . . financially. But Mother left me comfortably off.'

'What does he do for a living?'

'He's a . . .' Beth's eyes narrowed. 'Look, it's kind of you to call, but I am fed up with journalists and their cheeky questions and I don't have

127

to put up with being grilled in my own living-room.'

'Sorry,' mumbled Agatha.

James began to talk soothingly of Mary's work for the horticultural society and how much she had been liked by the villagers. Agatha took a covert look around. Mary's living-room had been altered already. The green wallpaper had been painted over, so that the walls were a uniform white. A lot of the little china ornaments which Mary had displayed on the mantelpiece and side-tables had gone. There were new book-shelves in the corner, or rather planks on bricks holding a great quantity of books. The green fitted carpet had been covered with faded and worn Persian rugs. The green curtains had been taken down and replaced with Venetian blinds. Beth or John Derry had tried to take as much green out of the room as possible.

'And are you a gardener yourself, Miss Fortune?' Agatha realized James was asking.

'No, I can't be bothered. I took all those plants out of the conservatory and got a friend in Oxford who likes all that sort of tropical junk to take them away. I switched off the heating. The conservatory will make a good study.'

'So you plan on staying here?' asked Agatha.

Beth gave her a hard look. 'Why not?'

'I assumed you would have rooms in Oxford,' said Agatha weakly.

'Of course. But these are the university holidays, or had you forgotten?' Beth suddenly rounded on James. 'Wait a bit. Did you say your name was James Lacey?'

'Yes.'

'I want a word with you in private. John, show Mrs Raisin out.'

There was nothing Agatha could do but get up and take her leave. Outside in the porch, John looked down at her. 'I've heard of you,' he said. 'You're the village Nosy Parker. Don't come round here again.'

Agatha walked off as stiff as an outraged cat.

When she returned home, her cleaner, Doris Simpson, was there. 'See, there's a bit in the newspapers this morning about Mrs Fortune's husband.'

'Rats!' Agatha seized the papers and sat down at the kitchen table and flicked through them. The American correspondent of the *Daily Mail* had interviewed Barry Fortune, Mary's ex. He was quoted as saying he was sorry to learn about such a terrible murder. He said he and Mary had separated amicably fifteen years ago. He had married again. He owned a chain of video-rental shops. If I had only checked the newspapers before I went out this morning, thought Agatha, it would have saved me from asking unnecessary questions.

'And here's your post,' said Doris, putting a small pile of envelopes on the table.

Agatha flicked through it. There was one from a lawyer's office in Mircester. The name was in prim black letters on the outside of the envelope, Carter, Bung and Desmond. Agatha opened it and her eyebrows rose in surprise. It concerned the late Mrs Mary Fortune's will. If she would call at their offices, she would learn something to her advantage.

'Come back, Doris,' she called.

The cleaner came back into the kitchen. 'I'm sorry for those kitties of yours, Agatha,' she said. 'Not much fun playing in that Gulag you've got out there.'

'Open Day's not far off,' said Agatha. 'The fence will be lowered then. You haven't told anyone about it?'

'Course not! What do you want to see me about?'

'This.' Agatha held out the letter.

Doris read it slowly. 'There's a surprise.'

'I wouldn't have thought she would have left me anything either.'

'That's not what surprises me.'

'What, then?'

'She didn't know you that long. I would think she would have already made out a will. Why change it to put in something in your favour? I mean, did she know she was going to die?'

'That's a thought.'

The doorbell rang. 'That'll be James,' said Agatha, still looking at the letter. 'Could you get it, Doris?'

The cleaner glanced at her quizzically. Normally Agatha would have rushed upstairs to put on fresh make-up or a clean dress.

When James came into the kitchen, Agatha handed him the letter. 'Oh, that,' he said, sitting down next to her. 'I got one of those this morning.'

'You might have told me.'

'I felt awkward about it, under the circumstances.'

'Anyway, what did Beth want to talk to you about?'

He stood up and closed the kitchen door and then returned to the table and sat down again. 'Mary had telephoned Beth earlier this year and said she was going to get married again . . . to me.'

'Ouch!'

'Yes, exactly . . . ouch. I have a feeling Beth regards me as prime suspect. Let's get out of the village and go to the lawyers'. By the way, why do you have the lights on in this kitchen and the blind down over the window? It's a lovely day.'

'Never mind that,' said Agatha hurriedly. 'Let's go.'

And so here I am again, she thought ruefully, running about the countryside with James, only this time it all seems rather . . . ordinary. And she congratulated herself on her new-found detachment.

The lawyers' office was down a cobbled side-street leading off the main square, where old buildings leaned towards each other, cutting out the sun. There was a faded lady behind an ancient typewriter in the outer office. They gave their names and were told to take a seat and wait. She retreated into an inner room. Dust-motes floated in shafts of sunlight that streamed through the window behind the desk. They were seated side by side on a horsehair sofa, a relic of the Victorian Age, like everything else in the musty office.

They were ushered in after a ten-minute wait. The fact that the lawyer who rose to greet them was comparatively young came as a surprise. Agatha had begun to expect an elderly gentleman with pince-nez and side-whiskers. 'Jonathan Carter,' he said. 'Please be seated. You are both beneficiaries under the late Mrs Mary Fortune's will. It is very simple and straightforward. I will not take up much of your time.' He picked up several pieces of stiff paper and flicked through them. 'I will only read the bit that concerns you both. I think you will not be surprised to learn that apart from a few bequests, the bulk of her estate goes to her daughter.'

Agatha felt a pang of guilt. Poor Mary. She really did like me. And I haven't even mourned her. All I could think of after we found her dead in that terrible way was to feel shattered because James confessed to having had an affair with her.

'Mr Lacey,' said the lawyer, 'you must understand that what is written here is in the words of Mrs Fortune. "To Mr James Lacey of 8 Lilac Lane, Carsely, Gloucestershire, I leave the sum of five thousand pounds in payment for services rendered, although said services were not really worth much."'

James said, 'Thank you,' in a stifled voice.

'"To Mrs Agatha Raisin of 10 Lilac Lane, Carsely, Gloucestershire, I leave five thousand pounds so that she may take herself to a reputable health farm to reduce her middle-aged bulk."'

'Bitch,' commented Agatha briefly.

'You will both be receiving the money in due course,' said the lawyer.

'I don't want it.' James's voice was harsh.

'Take your time,' said the lawyer. 'It is, I admit, a rather spiteful bequest. But do not reject it out of hand. We all need money.'

'Are you accepting yours?' asked James as they walked up to the square.

'Oh, yes. She's not alive, is she? I mean, money's money. You know, James, if she really was as bitchy as it now seems she was, it's not surprising someone bumped her off.'

'The world is full of bitches,' said James, lengthening his stride so that Agatha had to hurry to keep up with him. 'But no one goes about murdering them.'

'Let's go and see Bill Wong,' panted Agatha. 'And do slow down a bit.'

He stopped so suddenly, she almost cannoned into him. 'Why Bill Wong? He's told you to keep out of it.'

'But if we tell him about Mary's will, we might be able to ferret some information out of *him*.'

'I don't want to tell him about the will.'

'Don't you see, the police will know the contents of the will already. I'll tell him my bit. You don't need to come if you don't want to.'

He stood for a moment, his hands thrust in his pockets, rocking slightly on his heels, looking at his feet. 'All right,' he said abruptly.

They walked to police headquarters and asked at the desk for Bill Wong. He came down the stairs after only a short wait, a smile of welcome on his face. 'Just at my lunch-hour,' he said cheerfully.

'If you've got the time, lunch is on me,' said Agatha. 'We've something to tell you.'

'I hope you haven't been stirring things up with any amateur detective work,' said Bill.

'No, no. Do you want to hear our news or not?'

'I'd like lunch,' said Bill with a grin.

'We'll go to that restaurant James took me to the other day,' said Agatha briskly.

In the restaurant, she ordered a sirloin steak with sautéed potatoes, grilled tomatoes and peas. 'What happened to your diet?' asked James.

'Sod the diet,' retorted Agatha. She privately thought there was no need to go on suffering. She had no one to compete with and she was no longer romantically interested in James Lacey. Of course, she had read endless articles in women's magazines about how one should slim for one-self, one should feel good about oneself. But it had never worked that way for Agatha and she doubted if it ever would.

When they were served, Bill asked, 'Now what was it you wanted to tell me?'

'I'm a beneficiary in Mary's will,' said Agatha.

'I know that,' said Bill. 'And Mr Lacey here as well.'

'James,' he corrected. 'A very rude bequest it was, too.'

'Come to think of it, she must have hated us,' said Agatha. 'And why make such a recent will? She must have expected to live a long time.'

135

'Not necessarily,' said Bill.

'Why?'

'I don't want you getting involved.'

Agatha reached out a hand. 'I'll take that plate of steak-and-kidney pudding away from you, Bill Wong, unless you explain yourself.'

'Leave it alone. I'm hungry. Oh, I suppose the press will get hold of it. When her husband asked for a divorce way back when, she tried to commit suicide.'

'Emotional blackmail,' said James. 'Probably didn't mean to go through with it.'

'She would have done the job all right – bottle of barbiturates, bottle of vodka – but for one little miracle. A neighbour whose flat overlooked hers passed his day in watching the women opposite through binoculars, although he subsequently swore to the police that he was bird-watching. So he saw Mary swallowing pills and drinking vodka and swallowing pills until she slumped over the table and he called for an ambulance and the police. She was rushed to hospital and her stomach was pumped out. She was subsequently treated several times for depression, the last being when she was living in New York. She moved there after the divorce to a flat in Washington Square in the Village.'

'My cleaner, Doris Simpson, was about the only person who didn't like her when everyone else seemed to,' said Agatha. 'She said something like, "No warmth there. It's as if she's acting." Do you think that? Why come to the Cotswolds?'

'She is English,' pointed out Bill.

'Where from?'

'Newcastle originally. Her parents are dead. A lot of outsiders move to the Cotswolds. Take you two, for example,' said Bill.

'But don't you see,' said Agatha, pursuing her theme, 'she was acting being the perfect village lady, baking and gardening and so on. If she had lived, she might have tired of the act, moved somewhere else and adopted another role.'

'Speculation,' said Bill, shaking his head. 'I need more solid facts. I may as well make use of you while you're here. Let's start with the people who had their gardens ruined. Mrs Bloxby? Who would have a spite against Mrs Bloxby, of all people?'

Mary, thought Agatha suddenly, but could not voice her suspicions without betraying the confidences of the vicar's wife.

But another idea struck her. She said, 'James, do you remember when you were supposed to take me out for dinner in Evesham?'

'Very well indeed. That was the day I got food poisoning.'

'And that was the day you visited Mary!'

'What are you getting at, Agatha? I didn't dine with her.'

'But surely you had something to eat?'

'Let me see, coffee and home-made cakes, as I recall.'

Agatha's eyes gleamed. 'And then you were too ill afterwards to take me for dinner. I had told Mary you were taking me for dinner.'

'Wait a minute,' said Bill. 'Just hold it there. Are you suggesting that Mary put something in the cakes so that James would be ill and would not be able to go?'

Agatha nodded.

'That's ridiculous,' said James.

'Did she eat the cakes as well?'

James said slowly. 'No, she didn't. She said something about being on a diet.' In fact, what she had said was that she had no intention of becoming as frumpish as Agatha Raisin by letting her figure go.

Bill Wong's eyes were suddenly shrewd. 'I think you're suggesting also that Mary Fortune might have been the one who ruined the gardens. Do you know something about Mrs Bloxby, say, that you're not telling us, Agatha?'

'No,' mumbled Agatha.

He gave her a long look and then said, 'Okay. Let's start with you, James. Now the idea was that whoever ruined the gardens wanted to put competition out of the running. But let's just give Agatha's theory a whirl. Did you upset Mary before your garden was set alight?'

'As a matter of fact, it was shortly after I had told her the affair was over.'

'So let's examine the rest. Mr and Mrs Boggle?'

'Forget them,' said Agatha. 'They annoy everyone.'

'All right. Miss Simms, then, the unmarried mother who is secretary of the Ladies' Society.'

'We'd need to ask her,' said Agatha. 'She's not the type to irritate anyone.'

'And Mrs Mason?'

'The same,' said Agatha gloomily. 'Need to ask.'

'Mr Spott, he of the poisoned fish? I mean, if by some far-fetched chance Mary was out for petty revenge, then it need not be just plants.'

'Bernard Spott adored Mary,' said James. 'He would never have said a word to annoy her.'

'We're getting nowhere,' sighed Bill. 'I don't think your argument's got a leg to stand on, Agatha. Say one of those maddened gardeners decided to get revenge on Mary, which one can you see doing it? Mrs Bloxby, Miss Simms, James here, Mrs Mason, or the Boggles or old Mr Spott?'

'Must be someone from her family or her past,' said Agatha. 'Was the husband in America the whole time?'

'Yes.'

'But it must have been someone she knew,' said James suddenly.

'Why?'

'There was no forced entry. She opened the door to whoever. She was poisoned. Someone slipped weedkiller in her drink. What drink?' he demanded, looking at Bill.

'Hard to say, but from the contents of her stomach, brandy, I think. It was a strong measure of weedkiller.'

'And you've checked all the weedkiller suppliers?'

Bill groaned. 'Do you know just how many places in the Cotswolds sell weedkiller? Legion. But yes, we are getting around to them all.' Agatha had taken a menu from the waitress and was studying it. 'Never say you are going to order pudding, Agatha?'

'Icky-sticky pudding,' said Agatha firmly. 'Anyone else?' They all ordered the sticky toffee-syrup-laced sponge. Why was it, thought Agatha gloomily when she had finished the last crumb of pudding, that desserts like this, which could slip down her gullet in the old days without any effect, immediately made the waistband of her skirt as tight as a corset?

'I think the daughter is the best bet,' she said over coffee. 'Surely it's very simple. She inherits. She did it, or her boyfriend.'

'Her own mother?' protested James.

'She could have wanted it to look like the work of some maniac,' said Agatha.

140

'I tell you this,' said Bill, 'if it was a maniac, it might just have been some fellow who called at the door.'

'And she let him in and offered him brandy! Not likely,' said Agatha firmly.

Bill heaved a sigh. 'Thanks for lunch. I've got to be getting back. It might have been done by someone from her past and we'll never find out who it is.'

'Makes you want to forget about the whole thing,' said James after Bill had left.

'I think people will start talking soon,' said Agatha. 'We could start off by calling on Mrs Mason. She's a sensible lady. All we can do is keep on asking questions until we get a lead.'

Chapter Seven

At first, that afternoon, as they sat over tea and scones in Mrs Mason's living-room, it looked as if they weren't going to get very far. Mrs Mason talked in a hushed voice about 'poor Mary'. Both Agatha and James ferreted about in their minds for a way to find out what the chairwoman of the Carsely Ladies' Society actually thought about the dear deceased.

It was James, spurred to his own defence by Mrs Mason's murmur of 'You, above all others, must be grief-stricken, Mr Lacey,' who found an opening. 'I regret to tell you, Mrs Mason,' he said, leaning back in one of her velveteen-covered armchairs and stretching his long legs out in front of him, 'that although I am shocked and saddened by the murder, I am not grieving. I did not know Mary very well.'

Mrs Mason looked startled. 'But I thought . . .'

'I had an affair with Mary Fortune. Most people in the village seem to have known that. It finished a while ago. But despite that, I repeat, I did not know her very well and I am beginning to believe that she had a knack of putting people's backs up.'

'I think,' said Agatha quickly, remembering what Mrs Bloxby had said, 'that she had a way of making people ashamed of themselves and so nobody confided in anyone else what she had said or done.' James gave her a sharp look.

'Well, of course, put like that . . .' Mrs Mason adjusted her glasses and peered at Agatha. 'I thought I was making too much of it.'

'Too much of what?'

'She said, in the nicest way possible, that she wondered why no elections were held for the posts in the Ladies' Society. "Whatever can you mean, Mrs Fortune?" I asked. She smiled and said that she gathered that I had been chairwoman for several years and Miss Simms had been secretary. I pointed out that nobody had complained. "They wouldn't complain to you, dear," she said. "But there have been certain *murmurings*," yes, that's what she said, murmurings. "About what?" says I, getting sharpish. "Oh," says she as sweet as pie, "some of the ladies would like to see new blood at the helm." I found myself getting angry. "Like yourself?" I says, irritated-like. And she says, "Why not? Would you have any objections?" "Not me," says I, "but it's up to the group."'

Mrs Mason paused for breath. A red tide of colour rose up her neck. 'It would have been all right if she had left it at that. But she went on to say that the Ladies' Society over at Little Raddington had a very *presentable* chairwoman who was quite *young*.'

Her voice was a bad imitation of Mary's rather drawling accent. 'I bought myself a new pale blue twin set – you remember, Mrs Raisin, you admired it – and I wore it with my pearls to one of the last meetings. Mrs Fortune looked at it and gave a little smile and I suddenly wished I hadn't wasted the money. She had a way of smiling, she had, that seemed to say, "It doesn't matter what you do, you'll never look like a lady."

'I spoke to Mrs Bloxby, who told me that no one had been complaining about me being chairwoman. It was the opposite. She heard a lot of praise for me. She told me to think no more about it. But I said I thought Mrs Fortune would make a better chairwoman and Mrs Bloxby said, "No, that would not do at all." I was that riled up with Mrs Fortune that when I met her in the village shop, I says to her, I says, "I asked Mrs Bloxby if anyone had been unhappy with me being chairwoman and she said quite the opposite, so there!" And she looks at me steady-like and then says quietly, "Mrs Bloxby is such a *kind* woman," and o' course that made me feel bad all over again.'

'And how soon after that was your garden attacked?' asked Agatha eagerly.

'Wait a minute, I'll need to look at my diary.' She went to a veneered sideboard and drew a leather-bound book out from the back of a knife drawer. 'Let me see.' She rummaged through the pages. 'Ah, here's the bit about meeting her in the post office part of the village shop.' She flicked over more pages. 'Three days after that, it would be.'

Agatha flashed a triumphant look at James. 'But what's all this to do with that business about the gardens?' asked Mrs Mason.

'We're following up every lead,' said Agatha obscurely.

'So you're playing detective again?'

'I'm not playing,' snapped Agatha. 'I'm deadly serious.'

'You'll find it was one of those hooligans down from Birmingham,' said Mrs Mason. 'No one here would murder anyone for a few nasty remarks. Another scone?'

'The Boggles next?' suggested Agatha reluctantly. 'I mean, someone sprayed their roses black.'

'Must we?' asked James. 'It would be more a

case of the Boggles putting Mary's back up than the other way round.'

'I can't stand the Boggles either,' said Agatha, 'but it would be interesting to find out if their roses were attacked shortly after some sort of confrontation with Mary.'

'I think you're barking up the wrong tree, Agatha. All these attacks on the gardens were within days of each other. If they had been more spaced out, there would have been more of a chance to catch the culprit, but they all happened so quickly.'

'Let's try the Boggles anyway. Don't leave me, James. Boggle-interviewing means I need support.'

Mr and Mrs Boggle lived on the council estate at the end of the village. They had bought their council house and named it Culloden, not because either had any interest in the famous Scottish battlefield but because it was a name that had taken their fancy at the local nursery which sold signs for houses.

Usually people in villages have a soft spot for the elderly, and Mr and Mrs Boggle milked this sympathy for all it was worth. They did not go in for subtle blackmail; they demanded days out and trips to town from various people as their right.

'Now remember,' cautioned Agatha, 'if they want an outing, say both our cars are off the road. Go in for blatant lying, or they'll have us driving them to Bath or Bristol or somewhere. I took them to Bath once and it was a nightmare of a day.'

'I think this is a waste of time,' said James uneasily.

'I don't like them either,' said Agatha, 'but they're so blunt, they might turn out to be more useful than anyone nicer.'

James rang the doorbell, which gave a brisk rendering of the 'Post Horn Gallop'. Odd shuffling noises came from inside as of elderly animals shifting in their lair.

After what seemed an age, there were the sounds of bolts being drawn back and locks being unlocked and then the door was opened on a chain and Mrs Boggle peered at them.

'Oh, it's you,' she said. 'What do you want?'

'We want to talk to you about Mary Fortune,' said Agatha.

Mrs Boggle's elderly eyes gleamed with malice. 'Why not ask him?' she said. 'He must have known her better'n anybody.'

'Can we come in?' asked Agatha patiently.

'Soap's on. You'll need to wait till it's finished.'

The chain was dropped, the door was opened, and Agatha and James followed her dumpy figure into a fusty living-room where a television set blared from one corner. Mrs Boggle was layered in clothes topped with a woolly cardigan and print apron. Her husband, wearing an old shirt, a sweater and a cardigan and thick trousers, was staring avidly at an Australian soap. The room was full of the smell of old Boggle, a strange smell, not of the unwashed but of the decaying.

Agatha and James waited patiently until the soap ground to its syrupy end. It was one of those irritating episodes where a well-loved character has died and so there were seemingly endless close-ups of Australian faces swimming in tears. And why were the women all so tiny? wondered Agatha. What of all those goddesses one saw in films of Bondi Beach? Maybe the undersized female in Australia went in for acting.

When it was finally over, Mrs Boggle reluctantly switched it off. 'Well?' she demanded.

'What did you think of Mrs Fortune?' asked Agatha.

'Tart!'

Agatha stifled a sigh. 'I mean, did she upset you in any way?'

'Bitch!' muttered Mr Boggle.

'Perhaps you could tell us what happened.' James's voice was patient.

'Her had told Mrs Bloxby she wanted to help in the community . . . and it's no use you two expecting tea or coffee. I've got more to do with my savings.'

Agatha ignored this. 'Go on,' she said. 'Mary asked Mrs Bloxby how she could help out in the community?'

'Yes, so she told that Mrs Fortune to take us out for the day. The painted hussy called round here, mutton dressed as lamb, if you ask me.

'I said we wanted to go to Bristol to look at the ships. Didn't I, Boggle?'

'Yurse,' said Mr Boggle morosely.

'Her said, "Oh, come now, that's too far. What about Evesham?"

'I said, didn't I, Boggle, that it was her duty to help the old get about? I told her that not all of us had money to go gallivanting around in large cars. Yes, and I told her that the way she was going on with Mr Lacey here was a fair scandal. In my day, we got married, that's what I told her. I was never one to mince my words, was I, Boggle?'

'No,' said Mr Boggle, staring at the blank television screen.

'To which Mary replied?' prompted Agatha.

'That Mrs Fortune then had the cheek to say that we would be better off in the old folks' home than leeching off people. Can you imagine? Did you ever hear the like? I told her to get out and take her trollopy ways with her.'

'Have you any idea who damaged your roses?' asked James.

'Never had any doubt,' said Mrs Boggle. 'It was her, Mary Fortune. Did it out of spite. Knew we would take first prize with them roses.'

'But you didn't get a prize,' said Agatha.

''Cause we didn't have nothing left for the show to match them roses,' said Mr Boggle suddenly and violently. He leaned forward and switched on a large electric fire and a blast of heat scorched into the already hot room. Outside, the sun was blazing down out of a clear sky. The temperature must have been in the high seventies. The room was suffocating. The windows were covered in thick white net, and curtains which looked as if they had been made out of red felt blocked out what was left of the light. The very stifling air seemed to be full of years of shared marital venom.

'The wicked shall be cut down like the green bay tree,' Mrs Boggle quoted inaccurately but viciously.

'You mean you are glad Mrs Fortune is dead?' asked Agatha.

'Course. That one got what was coming to her. Unnatural to sneer at the poor aged like us. We never did get that trip to Bristol. We –'

'Good heavens! Is that the time?' Agatha leapt to her feet. 'Come along, James. Thank you for your time, Mrs Boggle.'

150

Seeing her prey escape her Mrs Boggle also got to her feet, but by the time she did that, Agatha and James had made their escape.

'Whew,' said Agatha. 'Wouldn't it be fun if it turned out they did it? At the back of my mind, there's always a fear that the murderer might turn out to be someone quite nice who was temporarily deranged by Mary. But who could feel sorry for the Boggles?'

'Mrs Raisin!' Mrs Boggle's voice sounded from Culloden. 'Come back. Boggle's fainted.'

James took a half-step towards the garden path but Agatha seized his arm. 'Running for the doctor,' she shouted back and set off down the street, with James after her.

'Are we going for the doctor?' asked James when he caught up with her.

'Waste of time. She wanted us back there so she could bully that trip to Bristol out of us. But I'll phone the doctor when I get home, just to be on the safe side. Yes, I know they've got a phone there, but it would be just like one of them to die to spite us. Come and have a coffee with me while I phone and then we'll try Miss Simms.'

Although he accepted her invitation, Agatha, still relishing her new freedom, realized that she would not have been devastated if he had turned it down.

She phoned the doctor, a new one in the village, a woman called Dr Sturret, and reported

Mr Boggle's 'faint'. Then she made coffee for herself and James.

'I'm beginning to wonder if there is anyone in this village that Mary hasn't riled up,' said Agatha.

'And it's all making me feel a bit of a fool.' James looked at her uneasily.

'Surely you have nothing to reproach yourself with,' said Agatha. 'Think of Mary as an easy lay.'

'I am not in the habit of thinking of women as easy lays,' said James crossly. 'Can we drop the subject of my affair? I'm heartily sick of hearing about it.'

'Okay,' said Agatha reluctantly, because there was still enough of her old obsession for James left to make her enjoy the trashing of Mary Fortune. 'When you've finished your coffee, we'll call on Miss Simms.'

'Why don't we call on Mrs Bloxby first?'

'Why her?'

'As the vicar's wife, she must hear a lot of gossip. And the women of the village will talk to someone like her more openly than they would talk to anyone else.'

'Maybe, after Miss Simms, if we have time,' Agatha pleaded.

'You know what, Agatha, I get a feeling Mrs Bloxby told you something and you don't want to tell me.'

'She told me something in confidence, James. It bears no relation to the murder. I can't tell you.'

'Fair enough. Miss Simms it is. Isn't she working?'

'Not any more. She stays at home and looks after the kids. The new man in her life is pretty generous.'

'It's amazing,' said James, 'how the ladies of Carsely not only accept having a blatantly unmarried mother in their midst but even make her the secretary of the Ladies' Society.'

'I think it's because villages have always accepted an unmarried mother or two in their midst before it became fashionable,' said Agatha. 'Let's go.'

Miss Simms answered her door. She was wearing the very high stiletto heels which she always wore, winter or summer. 'This is nice,' she said when she saw them. 'Come into the lounge and put your feet up. Gin? Lots of ice and tonic?'

'Lovely,' said Agatha, reflecting it was a treat to call on Miss Simms after such as the Boggles. Miss Simms was a pale, anaemic-looking woman in her late twenties. She had a long pale face and long mousy hair. She wore a short tight jersey skirt and a cheap frilly blouse, transparent enough to show a black brassiere underneath. Mrs Bloxby had told Agatha that Miss Simms was a competent and hard-working secretary and did a great deal of voluntary work in the village. Agatha found Miss Simms a very pleasant sort of girl. She had seen glimpses of her latest gentleman – a thick, beefy, florid man who drove off with her in the evenings.

'Are you investigating this murder?' asked Miss Simms after she had poured them drinks. She was sitting with her skirt hitched up, unselfconsciously exposing a border of frilly French knicker.

'Just asking a few questions,' said Agatha self-importantly.

'So what can you ask me?'

'We thought that if we could find out more about Mary, we could find out why someone killed her, and if we could find out why, we might find out who.'

'I know that line,' said Miss Simms. 'It was in *Morse*, or one of them detective things. Well, let me see. Mary . . . I didn't like her, of course. Sorry, Mr Lacey.'

'It doesn't matter,' he said gloomily. 'I'm beginning to think I didn't know her at all, although I can't get anyone to believe me.'

'I can,' said Miss Simms. 'I had a gentleman over in Pershore once. We had a few good times and then the police came around and said he'd disappeared with the firm's takings. He worked for Padget, the paper people. I was shocked, but could I tell them a blind thing about him? I said

154

he had a loud laugh and he wore his socks in bed, but the police said that was no good at all.'

'So what about Mary?' asked Agatha. 'I mean, I thought you liked everyone.'

'Usually. But that one got up my nose. She wanted to chair the Ladies' Society. I told her roundly we was all happy with Mrs Mason, but if she had any doubts about that, she could call for a vote. She said a few nasty things about Mrs Mason and I told her what I thought of her. No one criticizes any of my friends to me.' Miss Simms paused and took a birdlike sip of her drink. 'So then she got stuck into me.'

'What did she say?'

Miss Simms turned pink. 'Reckon as I don't want to say.'

'You mean what she said hurt.' Agatha looked at her sympathetically. 'You're not the only one.'

Miss Simms looked at her in surprise. 'I'm not? But everyone else said how she was an angel.'

'Because no one wanted to tell about the things she had said to them,' said Agatha. 'Come on, you can tell us.'

'I s'pose. She said that unmarried mothers like me living off the state should be shot. She said that if she got the chair of the Ladies' Society, the first thing she would do would be to find a more respectable secretary. I told her I took nothing off

155

the state. "You don't have to," she says. "You get the men to pay, and that's the same as being a prostitute." I said to her that we didn't all have money and the fact that she was doing it for nothing . . . Sorry, Mr Lacey. Anyway, I told her to get out and that was that. Do you know the next time I saw her, she was ever so nice to me that I began to think I'd imagined the whole thing.'

'This is dreadful,' said James. 'I never knew she was as bad as that.'

'That's us women for you,' said Miss Simms cheerfully. 'We always show the fellows our best side. Any idea who dug that big hole in my lawn?'

'No,' said Agatha. 'And the more I think about those attacks on the gardens, the more puzzled I am. It must have taken a great deal of daring, combined with a great deal of malice. It was dug on your front lawn, wasn't it? Anyone passing could have seen what was happening.'

'Fred Griggs asked all the neighbours and the people across the road, and no one saw anything,' said Miss Simms. 'But then, sometimes when I come back with my gentleman friend early in the morning, there's not a soul around.'

'What about your children?' Miss Simms had a boy of four and a girl aged two. 'Mrs Johns, next door, takes care of them,' explained Miss Simms.

'And she didn't see anything?'

'Not a thing. My gentleman friend, he's from the north originally, and he says that the air down here is so heavy that it makes everyone sleep like the dead.'

Agatha had to accept the truth of this statement. Any time she came back to Carsely after some time away, she found it hard to keep awake

'You weren't at the last meeting of the Ladies' Society,' said Miss Simms.

'I was busy,' mumbled Agatha. The truth was she had known that Mrs Bloxby had been going to ask for a volunteer to take the Boggles on a day's outing and so had not gone, fearing that the gentle vicar's wife would somehow, by her very presence, constrain Agatha to offer to drive the horrible couple.

'There's another meeting tonight,' said Miss Simms.

'I'll be there.' Agatha stood up. 'I think we'd better go. Anything to ask, James?'

He shook his head. 'I think I've heard enough.'

Outside, James said, 'So you won't be going to the Red Lion?'

'I'll join you there after the ladies' meeting.

What about rounding up the day with a visit to Mr Spott?'

'All right. But that one will have nothing but praise for Mary.'

Mr Spott's cottage, like Agatha's, was thatched. The external woodwork was painted bright harsh blue; window-frames, front door and fencing. It made the cottage look unsuitably garish, like a children's drawing executed in chalk colours. He had a small garden fronting on the road.

'The pond must be at the back,' said Agatha as James rang the doorbell.

Bernard Spott answered the door promptly. He was in his shirt-sleeves and gardening trousers, but his thin hair was as carefully greased across his bald spot as ever.

'Come in, come in,' he said.

They followed him into a pleasant living-room, low-beamed and with some fine old pieces of furniture.

'We have been trying in our amateurish way to find out what happened to Mary Fortune,' said James pleasantly. 'Strange as it may seem, Agatha and I feel we never really knew her and wondered if you had any insights.'

'It was a shocking murder,' said Bernard, 'really shocking. All that beauty and life extinguished in such a barbaric way.' He took out a handkerchief and blew his large nose in it with a trumpeting sound. 'It hardly bears thinking about.'

'How did you find Mary?' asked Agatha. 'I mean, being chairman of the horticultural society, you must have known her quite well.'

'Yes, we were very good friends,' said Bernard. 'She not only was a superb gardener, she used to bake me cakes and bring them round.'

'We have found,' said Agatha, 'that contrary to what we both thought, she was not all that popular.'

'You amaze me.'

'It seems she had a way of riling people up. Did you experience any of that?'

'No.' He looked bewildered. 'She was always kind to me.'

'To go on to another matter,' said James, 'have you any idea who poisoned your goldfish?'

'No, and our police force are inept, to say the least. I wrote to the chief constable to complain about Fred Griggs.'

'That's not fair,' protested James. 'Fred's a good man.'

'Tcha! What crime has he ever had to deal with? Those murders we had here before, it was the CID who solved them.'

'It was more Agatha here than the CID,' corrected James. 'Besides, the CID have been investigating the garden sabotage and they haven't

159

come up with anything, so it's not fair to blame Fred.'

'He knows the people in this village. He should have come up with something,' said Bernard mulishly.

'So,' said Agatha helplessly, 'you have absolutely no idea who might have poisoned your fish or who might have murdered Mary?'

'No, and if you will both take my advice, you will leave the whole thing to the police.'

'But you just said the police weren't doing a good job!'

He stood up as a sign that he wanted them to leave. 'I do not mind being interviewed by the police,' said Bernard. 'I accept that as one of the more unpleasant duties of being a British subject. Coming from you, however, it seems like vulgar curiosity.'

There somehow did not seem to be anything to reply to that.

As they walked away from the cottage, Agatha said, 'I'll find out what I can, and then I'll meet you at the Red Lion.'

As they turned into Lilac Lane, Agatha exclaimed, 'There's Beth waiting on your doorstep.'

They hurried towards her. She held out a couple of books as they came up to her. 'I just remembered my mother saying something to me about your interest in the Napoleonic wars, Mr

Lacey, and wondered if these books might interest you.'

'How very kind.' James glanced at the titles. 'Diaries! Where did you get these?'

'I borrowed them from the college. History is my subject.' She smiled at him suddenly and that smile gave her face something like beauty.

'Come inside,' said James. 'We'll have coffee.'

'I'd like that,' said Beth, 'but I would like to talk to you in private as well.' She looked at Agatha.

'See you later, James,' said Agatha and went slowly along to her own house, burning with curiosity.

She had just fed her cats when her doorbell rang. She was expecting to see James, come to report on Beth's visit, but it was Bill Wong who stood there.

'Oh,' said Agatha, that 'oh' being a little dying fall of disappointment. She reminded herself about her new-found freedom from emotional involvement with James and invited Bill in.

'I've come to ask you about Mrs Bloxby,' said Bill.

'Can't you ask Mrs Bloxby about Mrs Bloxby?'

'Don't be defensive, Agatha. I could tell she had told you something.'

Agatha stared at him for a long moment as she remembered something that Mrs Bloxby had told her, not about Mary's disparaging remarks or about the horticultural show; something she should have told Bill.

'I've just remembered,' said Agatha.

'I don't believe that, but out with it.'

'Mary got Mr Bloxby, the vicar, to take her confession.'

'Now that *is* something. Something must have been troubling her badly. I mean, the vicar doesn't normally take confessions, does he?'

'No, but he'll listen to anyone in trouble.'

'I'd better go and ask him. I wonder what it was about.'

It was about making a pass at him, thought Agatha, but there might have been something else there.

Bill left and Agatha prepared herself an early-evening meal. She wondered how Beth and James were getting along, and the more she wondered, the more she worried. Why had Beth, who had been so rude, done such an about-face as to offer books to her mother's ex-lover?

Chapter Eight

Bill Wong drove along to the vicarage. It was, he reflected, not like going to see a Roman Catholic priest. It had not been a formal confessional, surely, and the vicar was not High Church of England.

Mrs Bloxby welcomed him. 'I always expect to see our Mrs Raisin with you,' she said, ushering him in. 'What can I do for you?'

Bill stood in the shadowy hall of the vicarage. 'Actually, it was your husband I came to see.'

'Alf's in the church.'

'What is he doing?'

Mrs Bloxby looked surprised. 'Praying, I suppose. You can step over. He's never very long.'

Bill went back out of the vicarage and walked through the cemetery to the church next door. Huge white clouds were moving slowly above over a large summer sky. It was as if, during a good summer, the skies over the Cotswolds expanded in size, giving the impression of limitless horizons. Old gravestones leaned over the smooth cropped grass of the churchyard, the names faded long ago.

He went to the side door, pushed it open and walked into the warmth of the old church. The foundations were Saxon but the powerful arches were Norman. It was a simple church, with plain wooden pews and plain glass in the windows, Cromwell's troops having smashed the stained-glass ones. There was an air of benevolence and calm.

The vicar was kneeling in the front pew before the altar. What was he praying for? wondered Bill. For the murderer to be caught, or simply for his village to return to its usual sleepy calm?

As if aware of a presence behind him, the vicar rose and turned around.

'Mr Wong, is it not?' he said, walking down the aisle towards the detective. 'May I be of assistance?'

His scholarly face was gentle and kind.

'Perhaps we could talk outside?' suggested Bill, thinking obscurely that discussion of a nasty murder should take place outside the church.

'Very well.' They walked outside and sat down together on a mossy table gravestone, feeling perhaps that the last resting place of someone who had died no doubt respectably in his bed many centuries before was a more suitable place to get down to business. 'I suppose you want to ask me about the murder,' said the vicar.

'I learned that Mrs Fortune had asked you to take her confession.'

Bill waited nervously for a disclaimer or a demand as to how he had come by such a piece of gossip. But Alf Bloxby had lived long enough in rural villages to know that one has not much private life at all.

'Yes,' he said simply.

'You must understand that in view of the circumstances, I must ask you what she said.'

'I suppose you must. If there had been anything of the real confessional about it, I might refuse to tell you, but the matter is very simple. It amused Mrs Fortune to see if she could lay a priest.'

'Do you mean . . .'

'Oh, yes, what is it they say these days? She came on to me.'

'Are you sure?'

'I am not, I think, a vain man in that respect. We were in my study. She sat down on my lap and wound her arms about my neck and tried to kiss me.'

'And what did you do?' asked Bill, fascinated.

'I said, if I remember rightly, "Mrs Fortune, your figure belies your weight. You are, in fact, a heavy woman, and your weight is giving me a

165

cramp in my left leg." She got up and sat opposite me. I told her I had a great deal to do about the parish and so would she get to the point of her visit. She said she had sinned. I asked her in what way. She said she had been having an affair with Mr Lacey. The only reason I tell you this is because the affair was well known in the village.

'I pointed out that as Mr Lacey was a bachelor and she a divorced woman, what they did together was no concern of mine. I even ventured to lighten the atmosphere by suggesting she had seen too many old Hollywood movies. You know, where the heroine says, "Father, I have sinned."

'She became a trifle incoherent in her explanations, but I gathered that I was supposed to talk to James Lacey and suggest he marry her. Perhaps her time in the States had given her a rather naïve and old-fashioned view of what goes on in English villages. I said that whether he married her or not was entirely up to Mr Lacey.

'Mrs Fortune was a fascinating contradiction. On the surface, she appeared a witty and mondaine woman. After talking to her, I came to the conclusion that she was really quite stupid, a trifle common, and possibly mentally unbalanced. "Common" is probably an old-fashioned word. I do not mean she was of low class, rather that there was a streak of coarseness in her.'

'But would you say,' asked Bill, tilting back his head to look at a flock of pigeons wheeling over the churchyard, 'she would be capable of driving anyone hitherto considered normal to commit a brutal and fantastic murder?'

'Yes, I think she could.'

'Come, Vicar, do you mean to tell me she gave you murderous thoughts?'

'No, she embarrassed me considerably. What I have told you is mere speculation. My wife has not discussed her with me and yet I know my wife did not like her, and it is a very rare person whom my wife does not like.'

'So apart from making a pass at you and then wanting you to emotionally blackmail Lacey into marriage, she had no real confession to make? No darker secrets?'

'No, had she revealed anything of importance, I would tell you. People here talk about some maniac from Birmingham who might have come to rob her, but I firmly believe that one of the villagers is responsible.'

Bill smiled. 'No doubt our Mrs Raisin will be trying to find out who did it.'

'No doubt,' said the vicar drily. 'A most abrasive female, but there must be good in her, for my wife thinks the world of her.'

'Oh, there's a lot of good in our Agatha.' Bill got to his feet. He looked down curiously at the vicar, wondering if this cleric was as mild and gentle as he appeared on the surface.

'If you hear anything you think might relate to this case, Mr Bloxby, please let me know.' The vicar rose as well.

'Certainly.' He glanced at his watch. 'Time for tea. My wife makes an excellent tea. Perhaps you would care to join us?'

This last was said with such a reluctant politeness that Bill refused.

The vicar nodded and strode off in the direction of the vicarage. A man of iron, thought Bill, just like his wife, armoured in goodness against the likes of Mary Fortune.

Agatha sat down in the vicarage that evening and wished she had not come. The discussion was about gardens open to the public. Some of the villagers evidently made extra money for charity by serving teas. Agatha toyed with that idea and then rejected it. The fee for entry to each garden was twenty pence a head. Agatha had not thought before how much to ask and was depressed that her Great Deception was going to bring so little reward. She quite forgot that she was supposed to be putting out feelers to find out what they all thought of Mary Fortune, and became sunk in gloom. A stupid, childish trick was going to cost her six months of slavery for Pedmans in London.

By the time she went along to the Red Lion, she began to feel that it was just as well that she had been forced into going to London. There was no elation any more at the thought of seeing James. The more one learned about Mary, the more James became diminished in a way, because he had chosen to have an affair with her. The village in the quiet summer's evening felt alien and almost threatening. Agatha had that old feeling of being on the outside of life looking in. And what did she really know of the private thoughts and lives of these villagers? If the murderer was someone they knew and respected, would they not all band together to protect that person?

She would have been surprised could she have known that James's thoughts were running along roughly the same lines. He was feeling isolated as he stood at the bar, surrounded as usual by the easy friendliness of the locals, that peculiar village friendliness which was all on the surface and never really gave anything away.

He saw Agatha entering the pub and felt relieved. There was something very reassuring and honest in Agatha's pugnaciousness. When she went to join him, he bought her a gin and tonic and suggested they take their drinks to a table at the corner of the bar. Before, Agatha would have been highly gratified that he preferred her company away from that of the locals, but she could not get rid of the flat, depressed feeling that was assailing her.

'So how did you get on with Beth?' she asked.

'She was very charming. And very helpful with those historical diaries. She is a highly intelligent girl.'

'Where's the boyfriend?'

'He's gone off for a few days to see friends in Oxford.'

'Did she talk about her mother?'

'Only to say that they never got on very well and that she blames Mary for the break-up of the marriage. I invited her out for lunch tomorrow because I thought it might be a good idea to get to know her better and that way find out more about her mother. Care to come along?'

Suddenly Agatha, who had been so sure that she was free at last from any involvement with him, found her temper snapping. She got to her feet. 'Don't be so bloody naïve, James,' she said and turned and walked out of the pub. He sat and watched her go, wondering what on earth he had said to annoy her.

Agatha found the following day dragging slowly along. She could not think of anyone else to call on to ask questions about Mary Fortune. She had caught a glimpse of Bill Wong in the village the day before and she hoped he might call and give her some fresh ideas.

She made herself a microwaved lunch out of a packet of frozen curry, reverting to her old cooking habits, washed it down with a glass of beer, and had two cigarettes and a strong cup of black coffee for dessert. She could imagine James and Beth cosily ensconced in some pub or restaurant, talking about early nineteenth-century history, getting to know each other better. The girl was a pill, but James had been tricked by Mary Fortune, so who was to say he was not going to be seduced by the daughter?

The doorbell rang after she had spent half an hour amusing herself by playing with the cats in the garden. She glanced at the clock. Only two. Still, James might, with luck, have cut the lunch short.

But it was John Derry, Beth's boyfriend, who stood on the step.

'Oh, come in,' said Agatha, falling back a pace. 'What can I do for you?' He followed her into the living-room and slumped down in an armchair. He was wearing torn jeans and Doc Martens. There was something heavy and threatening about him.

'I thought you had gone away for a few days,' said Agatha.

'Obviously that friend of yours, Lacey, thought so too,' said John.

'What do you mean?'

'I met a smelly old woman in Harvey's, that post-office place, and she said something about us outsiders having no morals at all and that Lacey, having screwed the mother, was now out to screw the daughter.'

'I cannot imagine,' said Agatha, correctly identifying the culprit, 'that old Mrs Boggle would use that sort of language.'

'That's what it amounted to. What gives?'

'Beth and James share a common interest in history.'

'Is that what it is?' he sneered. 'I don't think your friend Lacey has any interest in Beth's knowledge of history. I think, along with you, he's the village snoop. Beth's got enough on her plate without being manipulated by a couple of middle-aged Miss Marples. Leave her alone.'

'Whatever happened to the modern woman?' asked Agatha sweetly. 'Is Beth not allowed to make up her own mind about who she sees?'

'She can't make up her mind about anything, the state she's in. Also, she's rich now, and I don't want any middle-aged Lothario chasing her to get his hands on her money or, for that matter, his hands up her skirt.'

'Bugger off, pillock,' said Agatha wearily.

He stared at her in amazement.

'You heard,' snarled Agatha. 'You probably murdered Mary Fortune yourself, come to think of it.' She stood up. He stood up as well and loomed over her threateningly.

'This is a nasty village full of nasty people,' he said. 'And an old wrinkly like you is one of the nastiest. Tell Lacey to keep away from her.'

'Tell him yourself,' said Agatha. 'Now get out.'

The doorbell rang. Agatha went to answer it, but he blocked her way.

'I haven't finished with you yet,' he said

The front door, which Agatha had not locked, opened, and to her relief Bill Wong walked in. He saw Agatha standing with her eyes blazing and her hands clenched. He saw John Derry glaring down at her.

'Trouble, Agatha?' he asked.

'Yes,' said Agatha. 'Mr Derry has just been threatening me.'

'Indeed? Well, Mr Derry, you come with me and we'll have a talk about this. Come along.'

John shouldered his way past Agatha. 'I'll get you for this, you old trout,' he said.

Agatha sat down weakly when they had gone. She then began to worry about her burglar-alarm system. It had gone on the blink while she had been away on holiday and she had done nothing about phoning up the security people. But part of the security system was that outside lights went on all around the cottage when anybody approached and she did not want her back garden floodlit when Roy and his men arrived to put in the plants. But right after that, she would get it fixed.

She turned on the television set and stared blankly at a movie, the kind which tried to make up for lack of script with exploding cars and blasting guns.

At first she did not hear the doorbell above the noise and then a sudden cessation in the shooting and screaming brought it to her ears and she scrambled to her feet and went to answer it.

'Why didn't you just walk in like last time?' she asked Bill Wong, who stood there grinning at her.

'The reason I walked in last time was because one of the locals said they had seen John Derry going into your cottage, and when you didn't immediately answer the bell I decided to let myself in. You always run to answer the bell, Agatha, and when you see me, your face always falls in disappointment, as if you were expecting someone else.'

'You're imagining things,' said Agatha curtly. 'Come in.'

She switched off the television and turned to him. 'So what did he have to say for himself?'

'Derry? He thinks you are an interfering old bag and that Lacey is either out to pinch his girlfriend or prove she murdered her mother.'

'That's mad. James and I only called on them

once. Admittedly James has been seeing more of her since then, but . . .'

'No doubt they have heard about your reputation for sleuthing. I warned him not to disturb you again.'

'You should have charged him!'

'What with? Yes, he says he threatened you. But I believe he's just a silly young man.'

'You won't say that when you find me one dark night planted in my own garden, upside down, and full of weedkiller. He's strong enough to have hoisted her up on that hook.'

'We're not sitting on our bums, Agatha.'

'So what do you know that I don't?'

'That the body has been released for burial.'

'When is the funeral?'

'At a crematorium in Oxford tomorrow. Don't have any mad ideas about going in the hope that the murderer is lurking in the bushes. We've promised Beth Fortune to keep it quiet. She says she doesn't want nosy villagers or the press.'

'What about the husband? Is he coming over?'

'No, he doesn't want to know anything about it. Miss Fortune is going to the States to see him during the Christmas holidays. There's your doorbell. No doubt that's Lacey returned from his lunch. I'll get it just in case Derry's been stupid enough to come back.'

He returned, followed by James. 'Well?'

Agatha greeted him. 'How did you get on? While you were romancing Beth, her boyfriend was round here threatening me and telling me to warn you off.'

'Why on earth would he do that?'

'He thinks you're after her money, among other things.'

'I cannot understand what Beth sees in a lout like that.'

'I do. Like to like,' said Agatha, turning her eyes away from Bill's sharp look.

'She is a highly intelligent girl,' said James stiffly.

'We don't seem to be getting very far forward,' said Agatha in a placating tone. 'I mean, I am beginning to think it must have been someone from outside the village, someone from Mary's past. If it wasn't the husband, then it could have been someone she had an affair with. Sorry, James, I meant someone else.'

'We're working on the American end,' said Bill, getting to his feet. 'I'll leave you two to discuss the case with the usual warning. Don't get involved and don't go around suspecting villagers and letting them know it.'

There was a silence after he had left. Then James said, 'I made notes on our interviews. Would you like to come next door and we'll go over them?'

Agatha had a sudden pettish desire to say

she would not. Damn Beth, she thought. Somehow Beth had reanimated all those feelings for James which Agatha thought she had lost. Competitiveness was a great part of Agatha Raisin's character.

'Wait and I'll get my cigarettes,' she said. 'You don't object to me smoking, do you?'

'I don't object to anyone smoking. I used to smoke myself.'

'You amaze me. Most of the people who've stopped are militant anti-smokers. How did you stop?'

'I got tired of it,' said James, who had actually given up smoking several years ago to please the then-current love of his life.

'I wish I could get tired of it. I don't even want to stop. Wait until I get the cats in from the garden. No, wait there!' she added sharply, terrified that James would see the bare garden.

'You're planning to surprise us all on Open Day,' he said. 'And yet you don't seem to spend much time in the garden.'

'I've spent all morning working on it,' lied Agatha.

In James's cottage some few minutes later, Agatha looked around, wondering not for the first time what it would be like if she lived there. And yet the living-room was comfortable, furnished with books and elegant old furniture. There was even a bowl of flowers on the window-ledge. She could not imagine putting her stamp on anything. James was that most irritating kind of bachelor, the kind who obviously does not need anyone to look after him.

He switched on the computer. 'I'm surprised you don't turn one of your bedrooms into an office,' said Agatha.

'I like to keep the spare bedroom free for guests,' he said. 'My sister and her children came to stay while you were away. Now let me see, I'll just flash this up on the screen.'

Agatha pulled up a chair beside him and read. Everything was neatly and accurately reported. 'If we were detectives in a book,' she said gloomily, 'I would stare at the screen and say mysteriously, "There is something there that someone has said which is not quite right." But all I can see is a lot of uninteresting twaddle.'

'Or I would say,' said James, 'that it must be Bernard Spott because he's the only one who said anything nice about her. Then I would go and make a citizen's arrest and have my photo in all the papers.'

'Did you really learn anything more from Beth about her mother?' asked Agatha.

'She said a bit curtly that she didn't want to talk about her mother, that Mary had made her, Beth's, early years hell with her tantrums and scenes. She seems very fond of her father.'

'If she is as intelligent and charming as you

178

say – although *I* didn't get that impression – then why get tied up with a lout like Derry?'

'I think he adores her and she needs that. Gives her stability.'

'Bollocks! You've been reading magazines.'

'Don't be rude, Agatha.'

'Sorry, but it did sound a bit like psycho-babble. I say, I wonder if anyone else got a sort of backhanded bequest in Mary's odd will. Why didn't we ask Bill Wong?'

'I asked Beth. We were the only ones so favoured.'

'How odd! I can understand her wanting to get at you from beyond the grave for dumping her. But why me? I was quite nice to her.'

'She was very jealous of you.'

'Why? You, me, because of our friendship?'

'A bit, but mainly because of your popularity in the village.'

'My *what*?'

'You're very popular, Agatha.'

'Oh,' said Agatha gruffly. She stared in a bemused way at the screen, not really seeing the words. Agatha Raisin popular! She felt quite dazed with happiness and gratitude. And then the temporary feeling of euphoria faded, to be replaced by one of dread. By cheating over this Open Day thing, she was putting such precious popularity at risk.

She got to her feet. 'I think I'd better make a phone call.'

He looked at her in surprise. 'Aren't you staying for a cup of coffee? I was just about to put the kettle on.'

'Put it on. I'll just make a call and come back.'

'Use the phone over there if it's that urgent.'

'It's private.'

'I'll go into the kitchen and shut the door behind me. I won't be able to hear a thing.'

But Agatha judged other people's actions by her own. Were the roles reversed, she would most certainly have pressed her ear to the kitchen door and listened.

When she got to her own house, she phoned Roy Silver.

'Aggie,' he cried. 'All ready for the planting?'

'No, I'm not, Roy, and I've gone off the idea of working for Pedmans. Tell Wilson to tear up that contract. No plants, no deal.'

There was a little silence and then Roy said, 'Your brain's become peasantified. There's nothing in that legal and binding contract which you signed saying anything about a deal, about plants. You can't get out of it, Aggie, so you may as well have the shrubbery. Come on, it's the best on offer. You'll knock them in the eye.'

Agatha felt herself weakening. 'Lovely blooms,' he coaxed.

'What if you're seen?'

'We'll be there at two in the morning and we'll be as quiet as mice. If anyone does see any movement, you can say you got some workmen in to lower the fence for the big day.'

'I suppose if I have to work for Pedmans, I may as well get something out of it,' said Agatha sulkily.

'That's the girl. Is it safe to arrive in that little shop of horrors down there? More murder?'

'The police are working on it.'

'See if you can solve it while I'm there and I'll get some publicity out of the reflected glory.'

'Anything to oblige,' said Agatha sarcastically and rang off. She went back to James's cottage.

'Everything all right?' he asked.

'Yes,' said Agatha uneasily. She sat down beside him again and tried to focus on what he had written, but her uneasiness about her garden would not go away.

She had meant to stop Roy's coming. For days she had meant to stop his coming. But as more and more people said they were looking forward to seeing her 'secret garden', the more Agatha felt she had to have something to show them. If she said there had been some sort of disaster and that everything had died and she was keeping the place locked up, some busybody was sure to think her garden had been vandalized like those others and tell the police and the police would say that it had been as bare as Mother Hubbard's cupboard when they had seen it.

So all too soon, in the middle of the warm dark summer night, there was Roy with his team of workmen and gardeners. They finished at dawn and drove off.

'Come along,' said Roy. 'You can't sit hiding in bed. Take a look!'

Agatha went outside.

A blaze of magnificent colour met her eyes. Flowers and trees and shrubs filled what had all too recently been a bare garden. The cats slid out round Agatha and frolicked on the grass as if they, too, were enjoying the display.

'It's magnificent,' said Agatha, awed.

'So now we can go and get a bit of sleep,' said Roy. 'When do the people start coming?'

'Not till ten. How do I tell them what flowers are what? I don't want to be exposed as a cheat.'

'See! Labels tied on all of them, nicely faded and weathered, but legible. You just bend down and read.'

They retreated indoors. Roy collapsed fully dressed on the bed in the spare bedroom and went instantly to sleep. Agatha took a last admiring look out of the window of her bedroom, set the alarm for nine and went to sleep as well.

* * *

At first they came in ones and twos and then suddenly Agatha's garden was full of exclaiming and admiring people. Roy, at a table by the side gate, collected the fees.

He could hear Agatha's voice describing the plants with all the authority of a real gardener. 'Yes, that is a fine example of a *Fremontodendron californicum* and that's a *Wattakaka sinensis*. Lovely perfume.'

And then Bernard Spott, to whom Roy had been introduced, raised his puzzled voice. 'But this is all wrong,' he said plaintively. 'Mrs Raisin, that is not a *Fremontodendron californicum*. That's a *Phygelius capensis*!'

Agatha gave a gay laugh and turned away from him to another visitor, but Bernard went on. 'And you said, Agatha, that that was a *Hydrangea paniculata Grandiflora*. Firstly, it's nothing like a hydrangea. It is, in fact, a *Robinia pseudoacacia* called Frisia. And this –'

'You don't know what you're talking about,' snapped Agatha.

'He's right,' came a woman's voice, a visitor to the village, a hard-faced woman in a straw hat and print dress. 'I would say all these flowers and plants have the wrong labels on them.' Her hard eyes fastened on Agatha. 'I've been listening to you and you do not know the first thing about the plants in your garden. *I* think you just bought them lock, stock and barrel from some nursery and the nursery put the wrong labels on them.'

There was a silence. Agatha was aware of Mrs Bloxby standing listening, of Bill Wong, who had just arrived in time to hear it all.

'Would anyone like some tea?' asked Agatha desperately.

People began to shuffle out of the garden until there was only Agatha, Roy, Mrs Bloxby, and Bill Wong left. 'Lock the side gate,' Agatha ordered Roy. 'What a disaster!'

'What happened?' asked Mrs Bloxby.

'I'll tell you what happened,' said Bill. 'Our Agatha has been cheating again. You did get all those plants from a nursery, didn't you? Just like you said you would.'

Agatha nodded miserably.

'That's no crime,' said Mrs Bloxby. 'A lot of the villagers buy extra plants and flowers and things to put in before Open Day. The nurseries around here do a roaring trade. It is only a pity that the nursery you went to proved to be so incompetent.'

'They're the best there is,' said Roy defensively. 'They'd never have got the wrong labels.'

Bill leaned forward and peered into a flower-bed. 'Come here, Agatha,' he said. He pointed downwards. 'I don't think any of your dedicated gardeners would tramp over your flowerbeds.'

In the soft earth was a clear imprint of a large booted foot.

'I brought men with me to put them in,' said Roy. 'Probably one of them.'

Bill turned to the vicar's wife. 'Could someone possibly have *switched* the labels?'

Mrs Bloxby put on her spectacles and went from plant to flower to tree, reading the labels. Then she straightened up. 'Why, how clever of you! That's exactly what is wrong.'

'Are you sure?' demanded Agatha. From inside the house came the sound of the door-bell.

'I'll get that,' said Roy, disappearing inside.

'I think that's what happened,' said Bill. 'Someone's played a trick on you, Agatha. When could they have done it?'

'It must have been sometime between, say, five in the morning and nine.'

'Daylight. Someone might have seen some-thing.'

Roy came back into the garden with James Lacey. Agatha groaned.

'You've done magnificently, Agatha,' said James.

'You may as well know the truth.' Agatha looked thoroughly wretched. James listened to the tale of her deception, his eyes crinkling up with laughter.

When she had finished, he said, 'You don't do

things by halves. All these months of hiding behind that high fence – I'm glad to see you've got it lowered at last – and all the lies and secrecy, and all for one Open Day in an English village!' He stood and laughed while Agatha stared at her shoes.

Mrs Bloxby's gentle voice cut across James's laughter. 'You know, I think it might be a nice idea to have tea out here among these lovely flowers and things. I see you have a little garden table and chairs there. I'll help you get the tea-things.'

Agatha, glad to escape from James's amusement, went inside with her.

Bill turned to James. 'Look, you're her nearest neighbour. Did you see anyone around this cottage this morning?'

'I saw a few people. Let me think. I was up very early. Mrs Mason has just got herself a dog. She came walking past and called out a good morning. I was tidying up my front garden. Then there was Mrs Bloxby.'

'What would she be doing along Lilac Lane?' asked Bill. 'It doesn't lead anywhere.'

'She often goes for a walk about the village in the early morning. Then along Lilac Lane, away from the village end, I heard a couple, a man and a girl, I think. I heard the girl laugh.' He stood for a moment, looking bewildered. 'That's odd!'

'What's odd?'

'I just remembered. The night Agatha and I discovered Mary had been murdered, as we were waiting outside her house to see if she would answer the bell, a man and a girl passed behind us on the road. I heard the girl laugh.'

'Why didn't you tell me this?' demanded Bill sharply.

'It slipped my mind. It didn't seem important. Just a village sound. I mean, they weren't coming away from the house or anything like that.'

Agatha and Mrs Bloxby came into the garden carrying tea-things.

James swung round. 'Agatha, do you remember that couple on the road the night we discovered Mary dead?'

'Yes,' said Agatha. 'I do now. I'd clean forgotten about them.'

'And now James here says he heard a couple at the end of this road this morning, early.'

'They could have been walkers,' said Mrs Bloxby. 'There's a lot of them about the Cotswolds. Although Lilac Lane doesn't lead anywhere. I mean, you can't drive anywhere, there is that footpath across the field at the end of it.'

'You were out early, Mrs Bloxby,' said Bill. 'Did you see anyone?'

'I only saw Mr Lacey's bottom. He was leaning over a flowerbed in his front garden, weeding, I think.'

'Do you think it could have been that Beth Fortune and her boyfriend?' asked Roy eagerly, who had been told all the details of the murder during the night by Agatha.

'I think I'll pay a call on them,' said Bill.

'Where exactly were Beth and John on the night of the murder?' asked Agatha.

'They were in Beth's rooms in college, studying.'

'Any witnesses to that?'

'No, but usually only guilty people arrange cast-iron alibis.'

'Come back when you've seen them and let us know what they say,' urged Agatha.

When he had gone and James, Agatha, Roy and Mrs Bloxby were seated around the table, James said, 'Even if it turns out that John Derry and Beth played a trick on you, Agatha, it's a far cry from murder.'

'Perhaps not,' said Agatha. 'I mean, surely the destruction of the gardens ties up somewhere and somehow with Mary's death. I wish I had never thought of this silly scheme. Now I have to go and work for Pedmans, the PR firm, in the autumn, and for six months, too.'

'I don't understand,' said Mrs Bloxby. 'How did that come about?'

Roy kicked Agatha under the table. She yelped, rubbed her ankle, and glared at him. 'I'm going to tell them,' she said. She explained about the deal.

'You must be very good at your job,' said Mrs Bloxby. She tried to surreptitiously feed Hodge, the cat, with a piece of muffin. Agatha had bought a packet of a product new on the market which promised 'real American blueberry muffins from your own microwave'. They tasted like wet cardboard. Hodge took it from her fingers and then spat it out on the grass. James crumbled his, so that his plate was covered in muffin crumbs. He hoped Agatha might think he had eaten some of it

'She is,' said Roy. Somehow Mrs Bloxby, without saying anything, was making him feel guilty about getting Agatha to sign that contract. Away from the world of PR, away from London, things which passed as normal business in the city had a way of appearing, well, shabby in this rural tranquillity.

He gave himself an angry little shake, like a wet dog. People didn't go about *planting* people in London; mugging, raping, knifing and shooting, but not *planting*.

'I think,' said Mrs Bloxby in her quiet voice, 'that the full enormity of Mary Fortune's death is striking me at last. Someone in this village is mad enough and deranged enough to have killed her and left her body in such a dreadful way. What on earth could she have done to engender such hate?'

'So you believe she was a murderee?' asked James. 'I mean someone who is going to get murdered because of some flaw in their character?'

How can you talk about Mary with such academic interest when you once made passionate love to her? thought Agatha. Aloud, she said, 'If only it would turn out to be an outsider!'

'You sound more like a villager every day, Agatha,' said Mrs Bloxby. 'I must go and look at some of the other gardens. Why, James, what about yours?'

'It's open,' he said easily. 'I do what the others do and just leave a box at the gate for the money.'

'Then I'll have a look. Agatha?' Mrs Bloxby turned to her. 'Care for a walk?'

Agatha shook her head. 'I couldn't bear the looks and whispers.'

'I wouldn't worry about it. Yes, they will most of them be laughing over it, but I think with affection. You are regarded as something of a character.'

'That's me,' said Agatha. 'The village idiot complete with cats. So where do we go from here?'

Bill came back into the garden. 'Until this murder is solved, Agatha,' he said, 'you should keep your front door locked at all times. Come to think of it, with that expensive security system in your garden, the lights must have been blazing while the men were working. Or did you switch it off?'

'It switched itself off ages ago,' said Agatha. 'I'll phone the security people and get them to fix it. What did Beth and John have to say for themselves?'

'John did it,' said Bill, sitting down. 'And he's quite unrepentant about it.'

'What!' screeched Agatha. 'Have you charged him?'

'It's up to you. But for a schoolboy trick? And have your deception come out in court?'

'But if he did that to me, maybe he did it to the other gardens. What was his reason for switching those labels?'

'He said he went out for a long walk because he couldn't sleep. He turned along Lilac Lane. As he passed your house, he saw the truck outside leaving. Wondering if it might be a burglary, because it was dawn and no one was about, he started to go up to the front door. He heard voices from the back garden and went to the side path and listened. He heard someone say, "So now we can go and get a bit of sleep. When do the people start coming?"'

'Roy,' breathed Agatha.

'And then your voice saying, "Not till ten. How do I tell them what flowers are what? I don't want to be exposed as a cheat." And then Roy here replying, "Labels tied on all of them, nicely faded and weathered, but legible. You just bend down and read." So he thought he would pay you back for "meddling in his life", as he put it, by switching the labels. He went down the lane a little and sat by the hedge and waited until the house became quiet. Then he went into the garden and moved all the labels around. I still can't think him guilty of anything else. He seems to me typical of a certain type of Oxford University student, boorish and somewhat sulky.'

'Damn him,' muttered Agatha. 'I would look a fool if this ever came to court.'

'Thought I'd let you know,' said Bill.

'How did the funeral go?' asked James. 'You did go to it, didn't you?'

'Yes, I was there at the crematorium. Very sad. Only me and two other detectives and Beth and John.'

'Some of us from the village should have gone,' said Agatha, suddenly conscience-stricken because all at once it was hard to think of the Mary who had been exposed since her death. She could only remember Mary's warmth and charm. Agatha suddenly became more determined than ever to see what she could do about solving Mary's murder. Whatever Mary had been, she had not deserved such a death.

Chapter Nine

Agatha remembered Bill Wong's warning when she was putting on make-up in her bedroom and heard her front door open the next day and someone walk into the hall. She was looking wildly at her dressing-table for some sort of weapon and seeing only the nail scissors when James's voice called up, 'Agatha, are you there?'

'Coming,' she yelled, and put some Blush Pink lipstick over her chin, swore dreadfully, wiped it off, and applied it properly.

She ran down the stairs. 'What's the matter?'

'I wondered whether you would fancy a trip into Oxford,' said James. 'I remembered this professor friend and phoned him up. He's at one of the other colleges but he's got us an introduction to a don at St Crispin's. I phoned him and asked him to lunch. That way we can find out more about John Derry.'

'And Beth,' said Agatha eagerly. 'Wait a minute. I'd better change.'

He looked appraisingly at her flowered blouse and plain skirt. 'You'll do. We're lunching at Brown's and no one dresses for that. I'll drive.'

And Agatha was happy as they drove off. She tried to persuade herself that she was happy because the day was sunny, because she was getting out of the village and ahead with the investigation. She did not want to admit that James's company was beginning to exert its old magic.

He took the road through Chipping Norton and Woodstock. 'Do you think anything will come out of this lunch?' asked Agatha.

'It might. I don't think either Beth or John Derry had anything to do with the murder, but we may as well try everything.'

'I wonder what he'll be like, this don. What's his name?'

'Timothy Barnstaple.'

Perhaps he'll be attractive, thought Agatha.

James parked in the underground car-park at Gloucester Green and they walked back along St Giles and so to Brown's Restaurant on the Woodstock Road.

'This is silly,' said James. 'I forgot to ask what he looked like.'

'Did you book a table?'

'No. We're meeting him now, at twelve, so it won't be too crowded, and it is the university holidays.'

They entered the restaurant and looked about. A thin middle-aged man got up as they walked in. He was leaning on a stick. He was dressed in a black jacket and black trousers. His black hair was greased back from a tired lined face. Porter from one of the hotels, thought Agatha and turned her eyes elsewhere.

But the man called out, 'Are you Mr Lacey?'

This, then, was Timothy Barnstaple.

'I took the liberty of ordering a drink while I waited for you,' he said. His voice was beautiful. In these days of the cult of the common accent, it was a pleasure to hear a well-spoken, well-modulated voice.

'I didn't know you were bringing Mrs Lacey,' said Timothy, leering at Agatha, 'but the pleasure is all mine.'

'Mrs Raisin is my neighbour and friend,' said James.

'And where is Mr Raisin?'

'I don't know,' said Agatha truthfully. 'I walked out on him years ago. I suppose he's dead.'

'Sit beside me, Mrs Raisin. But why are we so formal? What is your first name?'

'Agatha.'

'A good old name, Agatha. So sad the way they name girls these days. I have a student called Tootsy. That is her real name. She was christened that. A most scholarly girl. But how will she succeed in life? Her full name is Tootsy McWhirter, and she is a Thatcherite. Could not her parents write down, say, the Right Honourable Tootsy McWhirter and see how strange it might look? But we digress. I am very hungry. I will just order another drink while we look at the menu.'

The don ordered another double whisky and water and then peered over the menu. When they had ordered their food and Timothy had ordered a bottle of claret – 'We'll start with one bottle and then see how we get on' – he leaned his elbows on the table, pressed his knee against Agatha's and asked, 'How can I help?'

James told him briefly about the murder.

'Ah,' said Timothy, 'I read about that.'

'The thing is,' said James, 'we're just blundering about, finding out what we can about the characters of all the people close to Mary Fortune. What do you think of John Derry?'

'The college,' said Timothy, 'started to discriminate against the public schools, you know, Eton, Marlborough, Westminster, some time ago. Help the underprivileged and all that stuff. Down with elitism. The sad fact is that we have quite a lot of John Derrys, beer-swilling, loud-mouthed, at a loss at university, diligent enough swot at his comprehensive school, but not university material. Sort of chap who gets a bad degree if he gets one at all and then blames the capitalist system. Subsequently can't get a job and refuses to believe that turning up for interviews in torn jeans and a boorish manner has anything to do with failure. He latched on to Beth in their first year.

'Beth, on the other hand, is a highly intelligent girl.'

'So why get tied up with John Derry?' asked Agatha.

'The brighter the girl, the more sexually naïve. They think they are being feminist and liberated when they enter into a sexual relationship with some man at college, not aware that by funding him, washing his socks and making his meals, they are more in chains than their mothers. It's all sex.'

He pressed his knee harder against Agatha's. It was a small table. She moved her legs away and found them pressed against James's, apologized and moved them away again, where Timothy's insistent knee was waiting under the table to welcome her leg back.

The food arrived, solid English food. 'Do you think either of them could have committed a murder?' asked Agatha.

He held up a hand ornamented with dirty fingernails for silence and then attacked his food. He ate very rapidly, washing the meal down with great gulps of wine. 'Perhaps another bottle?' he said, breaking his silence at last.

James ordered another bottle and poured a glass for Agatha and himself before serving Timothy. 'Now,' said James, 'as I am sure you don't want to drink claret with the pudding, perhaps we can talk.'

But Timothy, it transpired, could eat apple pie and ice cream and double cream washed down with claret.

Agatha waited in silence and then said sharply, 'Let's get down to it. We brought you out for lunch to get a few facts.'

Timothy smiled dreamily at Agatha's pugnacious face. 'Dear lady,' he crooned. 'So forceful. I am but jelly in the hands of a forceful woman.'

He seized hold of Agatha's hand and kissed it. She snatched it away. 'Come on,' she snapped. 'Tell us more about John Derry.'

He drained the last of the claret and signalled the waitress. 'Perhaps a brandy with the coffee . . .' he was beginning but Agatha waved the waitress away. 'We'll call you when we need you. No brandy, Timothy, until you talk to us. Tell us more about John Derry. Any incidents in college involving him? He and Beth are in their final year when the term starts, are they not?'

He sighed and leaned back and lit a cigarette. 'There was an incident in John's first year. He beat up a fellow student in a drunken brawl. It never got to court. He was disciplined by the college.'

'What caused the brawl?'

'He said the student he had attacked had made a pass at Beth. Some witnesses said Beth had encouraged the advances and seemed delighted at the subsequent punch-up, egging John on to greater efforts. But I find that hard to believe. She is such a sweet girl. She'll get a good degree.'

He began to talk about college life, and time after time Agatha steered him back to the characters of John and Beth, but without much success. Reluctantly James ordered brandy for Timothy – 'A double, my dear,' called Timothy to the waitress – and said, 'The one thing we have got out of this is that report that Beth had incited John to fight.'

'Beth Fortune is no Lady Macbeth,' exclaimed Timothy, waving one hand expansively so that cigarette ash dropped into Agatha's coffee cup. He focused his tipsy eyes on James and nodded in Agatha's direction. 'What's she like in bed? Feisty, I'll bet.'

James sighed. 'I have not had that pleasure.'

'Why?' asked Timothy.

'Can we stick to the subject?' Agatha's voice was beginning to get a nasty edge to it. 'On the night of the murder, John and Beth claim they were in Beth's rooms. But the police say there are no witnesses to give them an alibi.'

'But there is a witness.' He tapped his nose and then stubbed his cigarette out in the remains of his pudding.

They both leaned forward. 'Who?'

'Me,' he said triumphantly. 'Of course, it should be "I", but I always feel one can appear a trifle pedantic if –'

'What are you talking about?' howled Agatha. 'What did you see?'

'I was crossing the quad below Beth's rooms on the evening of the murder. I looked up and distinctly saw John Derry and Beth Fortune standing by the window, talking.'

'At what time?'

'At about eight thirty.'

'Did you tell the police this?'

'They didn't ask me.'

'But you must have known that they were looking for witnesses,' said Agatha impatiently.

'I saw no reason for my evidence, dear lady. Such as Beth Fortune does not kill her own mother, and in such a gruesome way. Nor, for that matter, would John Derry. The manner in which she was killed suggests a brooding hatred. A real village murder.'

'What do you mean – village murder?'

'We don't go in for such colourful deaths in the city. Lots of inbreeding still in these old Cotswold villages, and witchcraft and all that sort of thing. Take my word for it, it's a village murder.'

His eye roved round the restaurant for the waitress and James, guessing correctly that Timothy meant to ask for another brandy, forestalled him by asking for the bill.

Agatha was glad to escape and take a deep breath of fresh air when they got outside. 'I thought we would be meeting a scholarly old gentleman,' she said bitterly. 'Do you think he meant all that, about being a witness?'

'Yes, I think he was telling the truth. Why should he lie?'

'Sing for his supper? Get more free booze out of you? When was the time of death exactly? Did we ask Bill Wong? We found her at eight o'clock.'

'I asked. They estimate she was killed about an hour before we arrived.'

'Why didn't I think of asking Bill?' demanded Agatha fretfully.

'Because we weren't exactly looking for alibis for people but more for reasons for killing Mary. Oh, God, think of the time it took to kill her and then to string up the body. He or she could have left only minutes before we arrived. And if John and Beth were seen at eight thirty, they could have had time to get back to Oxford, so they haven't really got an alibi, now I come to think of it.'

'Thank you for lunch, James. I should give you my share.'

'That's all right. Take me out for dinner next week and we'll call it quits. Are you going to give away the money Mary left you, Agatha?'

'No, I think I'll keep it.'

'Then you can afford to buy me dinner. Where now?'

'Back to Carsely, I suppose,' said Agatha. 'We might think of some ideas on the road.'

But nothing occurred to either of them, although they swapped various theories.

'Mrs Bloxby was right,' said Agatha with a shiver as they approached the village. 'The murder seems more awful the further one gets away from it. I think the shock of the whole thing has kept reality at bay.'

'There's the boy scouts' fête,' said James, slowing the car outside a field above Carsely. 'Want to have a look? They've got stalls and things, and I could do with some home-made jam. Mary used to keep me supplied. Damn it! Why did I have to think of that?'

'May as well have a look,' agreed Agatha.

He stopped the car on the verge and they walked into the field, admission twenty pence. Admission to everything in Carsely seemed to cost twenty pence. They wandered along the stalls. Mrs Bloxby, raising money for charity as usual, was selling home-made jam. Agatha and

James bought a jar each. James chatted away while Agatha edged off and stood waiting. She was still ashamed about her trick with her garden.

There were small boy scouts leaping about on a trampoline and boy scouts vaulting over a hobby horse. There was also a boy scouts' band playing tinnily.

Over in the corner was something that looked like a scaffold but turned out to be a 'mountain rescue' display. Three boys were hoisting a chubby boy scout up on ropes. He missed his hold and turned upside down and swung in the air.

'Just like Mary Fortune,' said Agatha with a shudder. 'Let's go.'

They turned away. A wind had sprung up and the clouds above were heavy and grey. There had not been rain for some time and little dust devils swirled up from between patches of bare earth among the scrubby grass of the field. There was also a faint chill damp in the air, heralding approaching rain. Agatha rubbed her bare arms and shivered.

Then, from behind them, they heard a familiar voice shouting, 'Harder, boys, harder! You're not pulling hard enough. I'll show you.'

Agatha and James stopped and turned round and looked back.

Bernard Spott had taken off his jacket and was

rolling up his sleeves to expose sinewy arms. He edged the boys at the 'mountain rescue' display aside and seized the rope and pulled one of the boys up easily. 'You see how it's done?' said Bernard. 'You use the strength of your forearms. Don't jerk the whole body. Just the forearms.'

'Walk away with me,' said James urgently. 'Don't show too much interest.'

'Why?'

'Because that's how it could have been done.' He put an arm about her waist and drew her along.

Good heavens, thought Mrs Bloxby, I do believe Agatha has succeeded in attracting James at last.

'Bernard? You can't mean *Bernard*. He's an old man.'

'But a very fit one. We kept discounting people because they weren't strong enough. But all any-one would have to do would be to bind her ankles with rope, leaving one long end, throw the end up over the hook, and pull the body up. Tie it up and cut the end.'

'Granted. But why Bernard?'

'I don't think it's Bernard,' said James, stop-ping suddenly. 'We've been arguing and think-ing and speculating for so long, I'm jumping to mad conclusions.'

They had reached the entrance to the field.

Agatha looked back. Bernard Spott was standing quite still, staring across the field at them.

'I say,' said Agatha, 'let's go to his house and wait for him. We could ask him if he knew of anyone else in the village who has his way with ropes. Don't look now, but he's staring and staring at us.'

'May as well try,' said James. 'But why not ask him now?'

'I don't know. I want a look at his back garden. We could even spot something the police have missed. I mean, they're not going to have searched the garden of a respectable old villager like Bernard very thoroughly.'

'I wish I'd never mentioned Bernard,' said James peevishly. 'I've had enough of this for one day.'

'Then drop me off,' said Agatha. 'I'll go on my own.'

'Oh, in that case I'd better go with you in case you make a fool of yourself,' said James ungraciously. 'Must you smoke?' he demanded, as Agatha lit a cigarette as soon as she was in the car.

'I thought you didn't mind people smoking.'

'So I lied.'

Agatha tossed the lit cigarette out of the car window.

He had moved off as he was speaking, but he immediately slammed on the brakes. 'Of all the stupid things to do, Agatha. The ground's as dry as tinder. You could set the countryside alight.'

Agatha stayed in the car, a mulish look on her face, as he searched the ditch until he had found her discarded cigarette and put it out. He had no right to speak to her in that tone of voice.

'You're a male chauvinist pig,' she said as soon as he got back in.

'And you, my dear Agatha, are the greatest female chauvinist sow it has ever been my ill luck to come across.'

'Oh, sod you, James, and bugger the country-side and all who sail in her. Are we going to Bernard's or not?'

'I've a good mind not to go. Do you know what? We're being childish even thinking that old man could do such a thing.'

'I didn't like the way he was looking at us,' said Agatha.

'Woman's intuition?'

'Something like that, James dear.'

'So what are you going to do if he comes back while we are ferreting around, looking for God knows what? Point a finger at him and say, "You did it!" and he will break down and say, "Mea culpa, O great detective lady"?'

'Why are you so beastly angry all of a sudden?' demanded Agatha.

There was a silence while he steered the car round a corner and then up the hill to Bernard's cottage. 'I don't know,' he said in a mild voice. 'I really don't know.'

'Well, figure it out next time before you open your trap,' said Agatha, still ruffled. When the car stopped she got out and went up the garden path and round the side of Bernard's house to the back.

James sat tapping the wheel and watching her disappear. Then he shrugged and got out as well and followed her.

The sky above was growing darker. Little snatches of sound from the scouts' band filtered to his ears. He went round the side of the cottage. The back garden was quite large, heavy with the scent of roses. A sharp wind sent a drift of blossom scattering over the grass. In the middle of the garden was a round pond where goldfish darted here and there in the greenish water.

Agatha turned and saw him and said in a quiet voice, 'Come here and look at this.'

He went to join her. There was a square patch of bare, well-raked earth planted with neat little wooden crosses. On each cross was a carved name, Jimmy, William, Harry, George, Fred, Alice, Emma, Olive, and so on.

'Animals' cemetery?' asked James.

'Do you know what I think those are?' said Agatha. 'I think they're the graves of those goldfish that were poisoned.'

'Come on, Agatha. Nobody gives names to goldfish.'

'I think he did. There's one way to find out.' She bent down and started digging in the earth with her fingers.

'Stop that, Agatha,' said James. 'It'll be a cat.'

'Then, if all these graves are animals, there's still something up with him. Aha!' She straightened up and pointed downwards. The remains of a nearly decomposed goldfish lay unearthed. 'Don't you see?' she said, her eyes gleaming. 'If he was as potty as this about a lot of goldfish and if Mary poisoned them and he knew about it, it could have turned his brain.'

They both stiffened as they heard the front-garden gate squeal on its hinges. 'Cover that up, quick,' said James.

'No,' said Agatha. She turned to face the entrance to the back garden. Bernard came round the corner of the house, his jacket over his arm. He stopped short at the sight of them for a moment and then walked quickly up to them. He looked down at the open grave at Agatha's feet and said in a quiet voice, 'Why have you desecrated Jimmy's grave?'

'You killed Mary,' said Agatha in a flat voice. 'You discovered she'd poisoned your fish and so you killed her.'

'Oh, really, so where are the police, Agatha?'

'They'll be here any moment,' said Agatha, moving behind James for protection. She improvised wildly. 'The forensic people traced that rope to you.'

'That's not possible,' he said. Then, as if realizing that by remark he had given himself away, he sat down suddenly on the grass.

'Why did you do it?' asked James.

'She humiliated me,' said Bernard, his head bowed. 'She flirted with me and when I made a pass at her, she laughed in my face and called me a silly old man. I was furious. I told her that she had deliberately led me on to make a fool of me and that I would tell everyone so. But of course I didn't. It would make me look too ridiculous, a man of my age.

'I heard a movement in the garden. The old do not sleep heavily. I looked out. There was bright moonlight. I saw her bending over the pond. I did not go out. I had become frightened of her, frightened she would laugh and jeer at me. But I found my goldfish dead in the morning, all my friends, my pets, my family. I used to sit by the pond and talk to them. I could think of nothing else but punishing her.

'It was surprisingly easy. The next time I saw her in the intervening weeks, she was easy and friendly with me, as if nothing had happened. She even called round, bringing me a cake. So I made my preparations. I called on her and asked her for a drink. I said I would like brandy, knowing that she often liked a glass of brandy. When she had poured two glasses, I said I thought I heard someone moving outside. When she went off to look out of the window, I put the poison in her glass.

'I had an agonizing time wondering whether she would drink it or not. At last I said when I was in the navy we used to drink our brandy down in one go, but I couldn't expect a lady to be able to do that. She laughed and said, "Why not?" and tipped the contents of her glass down her throat.

'I watched her die. I felt nothing at all. Nothing. I hadn't yet touched my own drink. I poured it carefully into the bottle after I had pulled on a pair of gloves, and then put the top back on the bottle. I put my own glass in my pocket, along with the one she had drunk out of, to take away with me. I sponged the vomit from her mouth off the carpet. I knew traces of it would be found by the police, but I did not want to make matters easy for them.

'I lifted her up . . . and well, the rest you know. I wanted her to be found desecrated, the way she had desecrated those gardens and in revenge for killing my fish. I knew she was the one who had tried to destroy the other gardens. She was mad.'

'I'll see if the police have arrived,' said Agatha in a thin voice.

She ran from the garden, round the front and to the cottage next door, where she screamed at the startled lady, a Mrs Bain, to let her use the phone. She called Fred Griggs and then went back reluctantly to join James and Bernard.

But when she reached the back garden, James was alone.

'Poor mad old man,' said James. 'He's gone in to lock up a few things before the police take him away.'

At that moment, Bernard reappeared. 'I'll just feed my new family before I go,' he said. He crossed to the goldfish pond. With a sigh of relief, Agatha heard the wail of a police siren in the distance.

James suddenly put his arms around her and she gratefully leaned against him and buried her face in his chest. 'That's that,' came Bernard's now quavering voice. 'I'll just get something from the kitchen.'

Agatha raised her head. 'You should go with him. He might run away.'

'We'd better go in anyway. The police will be hammering at the front door.'

They went in by the kitchen door. Sure enough, there was banging on the door. Agatha opened it and Bill Wong and two detectives came in. 'We got your message on the police radio. Where is he?'

Agatha looked wildly around. 'I don't know. Somewhere.'

And then a drumming sound reverberated down from the ceiling overhead.

Bill and his colleagues raced for the stairs. James pulled Agatha back. 'Don't go,' he said. 'It won't be pretty.'

'What do you mean?'

'I think he poisoned his new fish – and then he poisoned himself. They may be able to pump him out in time, but I doubt it.'

Upstairs, radios crackled as they called for an ambulance. 'Let's go and sit in the garden, Agatha,' said James. 'There's nothing more we can do here.'

Epilogue

It was two days after the death of Bernard Spott. The rain, which had broken the long spell of good weather, had ceased and the sun once more shone down.

Agatha and James were sitting in Agatha's garden. James was enthusiastic about the flowers and bushes, so much so that Agatha was almost able to forget about her deception. They had been questioned separately and this was the first time they had got together since they had discovered that Bernard was the murderer.

'Why did you let him go off alone into the house?' asked Agatha. 'Did you guess he would take his own life?'

'I thought he might. He was a brave man during the war. As soon as I heard that awful drumming sound upstairs, I knew it was his heels drumming on the floor after a swig of poison. He poisoned his new fish as well. I should have kept an eye on him and let him

213

stand trial. My only excuse is that I was so shocked and upset, I didn't really know what I was doing.'

'He may have been a brave man,' said Agatha sharply, 'but he committed a most dreadful crime and should have stood trial for it.'

Bill Wong appeared around the side of the house, Agatha having no reason to lock the gate any more.

He sat down and studied them for a few moments and then said, 'We were almost on to Bernard, you know.'

'You're just saying that,' said Agatha.

'No, we had been scouring the nurseries far and wide for someone who might have bought that particular brand of weedkiller around the time of the murder.'

'What brand?'

'Clean Garden. An innocuous name for some quite lethal stuff.'

'But lots of people buy it, surely?'

'We had photographs of people in this village, even you pair, which we had taken when you weren't looking. We showed them around the nurseries, and right over in darkest Oxfordshire they recognized Bernard Spott. That and his navy background and the fact that he was once a keen yachtsman made him look like our man. The knots on that rope had been done by an expert.' He looked at their outraged faces and laughed. 'Don't worry. I'm not taking the credit away from you. We had no real proof. What put you on to him? I mean, you said you had watched him helping the boy scouts, but surely that wasn't enough.'

'It was the graves in his garden,' said Agatha.

'Graves? What graves?'

'All those little graves for his poisoned fish, all with crosses and names.'

'We saw those,' said Bill. 'But we asked him and he explained it was part of his garden which he reserved as an animals' cemetery, and when anyone in the village had a dead cat or dog, they brought it to Bernard. But what I cannot understand is why you two gave him time to poison himself.'

James flashed a warning look at Agatha. 'We were in shock,' he said blandly. 'We did not think he would take his own life.'

Bill gave a little sigh and clasped his tubby hands over his chest. 'Mad. All mad. What exactly was up with Mary Fortune, I doubt we'll ever know. She was diagnosed in America as being depressed, which seems to cover a multitude of mental ailments.' He looked at James. 'Why it was you never suspected anything was wrong with her, considering the circumstances, is beyond me.'

'Even Agatha here did not know she was that deranged,' said James. 'Look, she seemed a flirtatious, easy-going woman out for a good time, with no strings attached. When she was quite foul to me when I broke it off, I felt so guilty about having misunderstood her – by that I mean that it had never crossed my mind before that she was considering marriage to me – I felt guilty. Then, as other people might have told you, and even Bernard told us, she could be really nasty and then, the next time you met her, so warm and charming, it was as if you had imagined it all.'

'And Beth and John are completely in the clear.' Agatha sounded as if she regretted that fact. 'I suppose the dreadful couple will be settling in the village.'

'No, they're putting the house up for sale,' said Bill. 'I expected to see your pictures all over the newspapers, Agatha – "Village Sleuth Strikes Again".'

'I thought you might have told them it was I who solved your bloody murder,' said Agatha peevishly.

'Not my decision. My superiors seem to have carefully omitted that fact when they spoke to the press.'

Agatha looked huffy. 'You would think, with my reputation, they would have called round here.'

Bill smiled. 'You've still got time to let them know it was you.'

'Too late,' said Agatha, wise in the ways of newspapers. 'The story is dead already. That find of two headless corpses in Birmingham knocked it off the pages. If I step in now, they'll just think I'm some bragging old trout trying to get in on the act.'

'You forget,' put in James, 'that if it hadn't been for me, you wouldn't have got on to Bernard in the first place.'

Agatha's bearlike eyes fastened on him 'What had you got to do with it? Yes, you did say it was Bernard and then immediately went back on it and if I hadn't insisted on going, if I, I repeat, I hadn't discovered those graves and dug one up, he'd still be at liberty.'

'I doubt it,' said Bill. 'We found a neatly typed and signed confession to the murder in his desk. It was addressed to police headquarters in Mircester. He'd probably have sent it to us soon enough.'

'Well, I think I did brilliantly,' said Agatha, 'and if I don't say so, who else is going to? Oh, here's Mrs Bloxby. Mrs Bloxby . . .'

'Margaret.'

'Margaret, I mean. I solve this murder and James and Bill are trying to take the credit away from me.'

Mrs Bloxby sat down. 'Such a sad affair. And Bernard had been in this village for quite a long time. Who would have thought it? One never really knows what goes on inside people's brains. I went up to Bernard's after his fish had been poisoned to sympathize with him and he shrugged and said, "They were only fish. I can get more." Bernard Spott was one of the fixtures of the village that no one ever really thought much about. He has a sister, a spinster of seventy-five, called Beryl Spott, who has inherited the cottage. I must warn you, Agatha, that she has already visited the vicarage to say she intends to reside here.'

'Why warn me?'

'She is convinced that her brother was innocent and that you, Agatha, hounded him to his death.'

'Just as well I'm going to London.'

'Must you?' Mrs Bloxby looked at her sympathetically. 'Have you a copy of the contract? There might be some clause in it letting you off the hook due to illness or something like that. I mean, if you were ill, you could not go.'

Agatha brightened. 'I'll go and get it. Roy sent me a copy.'

She went into the house and a short time later returned with the contract. She bent over it and scanned every line and then sighed. 'No let-out that I can see. I'd better just go and get it over with. It might be fun to be back in harness.'

'You could fail miserably and be a rotten PR,'

said Bill, 'and then they would be glad to send you home.'

'I couldn't do that,' exclaimed Agatha. 'My pride wouldn't let me. What about my poor cats, Hodge and Boswell, locked up for six months in a London flat?'

'I'll take them,' said James suddenly. 'I like cats. I'll look after them until you come back.'

'Thank you,' said Agatha. 'I'd feel better about things knowing they were with you.' She brightened. If James had her cats, then she would have plenty of excuses to phone him up to ask how they were.

'And you will be able to come down at weekends, surely,' said Mrs Bloxby.

Agatha shook her head. 'They'll work me to death. It'll be weekends as well most of the time.'

'I'll take care of your garden,' said Mrs Bloxby 'It's so lovely, and by the time you return, spring will be here again.'

Agatha had a sudden thought. 'Did you ever find out about that couple, Bill? You know, the ones we heard out on the road the night Mary was murdered.'

'Oh, them, it's hard to believe. After we learned about them, we put out an appeal on television for them to come forward, without any success. Then, after the solution to the murder had been reported in yesterday's papers, they walked into the police headquarters as bold as brass.'

'Who are they?' asked James. 'Why didn't they come forward before?'

'It was a young fellow who lives on the council estate, Harry Trump, and his girlfriend from Evesham, Kylie Taylor. When asked why they hadn't come forward before, they said that you could never trust the police and we might have pinned the murder on them. I must go. Call in and see me before you leave for London, Agatha.'

'There's some time to go before then,' said Mrs Bloxby, getting to her feet as well.

After they had left, James said, 'I'd better be getting along. See you in the Red Lion later, Agatha, and don't forget you owe me dinner.'

He bent down to kiss her cheek, but at that moment she turned her head and the kiss landed full on her mouth, a mouth which was warm and tingling. As James straightened up, Agatha looked up at him in a dazed way.

'Goodbye,' he said abruptly and strode out of the garden.

Agatha could not quite believe those last weeks before her departure for London. It was like the bad old times. James was polite to her when she met him in the pub, but quite distant. She invited him out for dinner several times but he always had an excuse ready. She began to long for her departure as much as she had so recently dreaded it.

At last the day arrived and she delivered her cats to James. She had already said goodbye to her other friends. She stood in James's hallway, the cat baskets at her feet, and said awkwardly, 'I'm off, then.'

'Have a good time,' he replied.

'I'll phone.'

'Yes, of course.'

'Well, er, goodbye.'

'Goodbye, Agatha.' He held open the door for her.

Agatha went out stiffly to her car and climbed in. She drove off without looking out of the window. James watched her go. He should not have been so cold towards her but that kiss had alarmed him. He wondered if he would ever get over the shame of his affair with Mary Fortune. He did not even want to think of any emotional entanglement. Perhaps once he was feeling better about himself, he might travel up one day and take her out to lunch. He went back in and stared at the computer screen. It was a cold, windy day and leaves were swirling down from the trees outside.

The horror had left the village and Carsely was settling down for its long winter sleep, safe and calm and untroubled. And boring, he thought dismally, half his mind still occupied with that forlorn figure of Agatha getting into her car.

Agatha arrived at Pedmans at Cheapside on the Monday. The receptionist took a note of her name and phoned upstairs. Then she smiled at Agatha. 'Your secretary, Peta, will be down in a minute.'

But Agatha waited a whole ten minutes before a lank girl in an Armani trouser suit drifted down the stairs.

'Oh, there you are, sweetie,' Peta said by way of greeting. 'Follow me and I'll show you to your sanctum.'

Agatha grimly followed her. She looked around a small dark office and bared her teeth. 'Let's get one thing straight, Peta,' she said. 'When you have informed Mr Wilson that this office is an insult and found me a better one, you will remember to never dare call me sweetie again. I am Mrs Raisin to you at all times. And when you've finished doing that, get me a cup of coffee.'

Peta made a brave stand. 'We all get our own coffee in this firm. Secretaries are not waitresses, you know.'

'Just do it,' barked Agatha, 'or find yourself another boss. Jump to it!'

And Peta jumped.

A short time afterwards, Agatha was ensconced

in a larger office while Peta silently placed a tray of coffee and biscuits in front of her.

For one brief moment, Agatha thought of James, of Mrs Bloxby, of her cats, her home, her garden, and closed her eyes in pain.

Then she opened them again and pulled the phone towards her.

She was back in business and there was work to be done.

Carsely could wait.

No. of copies	Order	Title	RRP	Total
		Agatha Raisin and the Quiche of Death	£5.99	
		Agatha Raisin and the Vicious Vet	£5.99	
		Agatha Raisin and the Walkers of Dembley	£5.99	
		Agatha Raisin and the Terrible Tourist	£5.99	
		Agatha Raisin and the Murderous Marriage	£5.99	
		Agatha Raisin and the Perfect Paragon	£17.99	
		Grand Total		**£**

Please feel free to order any other titles that do not appear on this order form!

Name: _____

Address: _____

_____ Postcode: _____

Daytime Tel. No. / Email _____
(in case of query)

Three ways to pay:
1. *For express service telephone the TBS order line on 01206 255 800 and quote 'CRBK'. Order lines are open Monday–Friday, 8:30am–5:30pm*

2. I enclose a cheque made payable to **TBS Ltd** for £ _____

3. Please charge my ☐ Visa ☐ Mastercard ☐ Amex ☐ Switch

   (Switch issue no. _____)

   Card number: _____

   Expiry date: _____ Signature _____
   (your signature is essential when paying by credit card)

Please return forms (*no stamp required*) to, FREEPOST RLUL-SJGC-SGKJ, Cash Sales / Direct Mail Dept, The Book Service, Colchester Road, Frating, Colchester CO7 7DW.

Enquiries to readers@constablerobinson.com
www.constablerobinson.com

Constable and Robinson Ltd (directly or via its agents) may mail, email or phone you about promotions or products.
☐ Tick box if you do not want these from us ☐ or our subsidiaries